Queen in the Shadows

Also by Liz van Santen

The Unfinished Symphony of Love
The Humble Pawn

Queen in the Shadows is the second novel
in *The Humble Pawn* duology.
Both can be read as standalone novels.

Queen in the Shadows

Liz van Santen

The
Book
Guild

First published in Great Britain in 2025 by
The Book Guild Ltd
Unit E2 Airfield Business Park,
Harrison Road, Market Harborough,
Leicestershire. LE16 7UL
Tel: 0116 2792299
www.bookguild.co.uk
Email: info@bookguild.co.uk
X: @bookguild

The manufacturer's authorised representative in the
EU for product safety is Authorised Rep Compliance Ltd,
71 Lower Baggot Street, Dublin D02 P593 Ireland (www.arccompliance.com)

This work is entirely fictitious and bears no resemblance to any persons living or dead.

Typeset in 11pt Minion Pro

Printed and bound in Great Britain by 4edge Limited

ISBN 978 1835742 297

British Library Cataloguing in Publication Data.
A catalogue record for this book is available from the British Library.

For strong women everywhere.

Looks can't hide your true identity. It's the eyes that give you away... the soul behind them. The intent. The shadows.
Vicki Peterson

Prologue

She blinked her eyes against the horror of darkness. She could not rid herself of her terrifying nightmare. The sins of the past. She saw his body, bound to the bed; lifeless; his skin pale, almost translucent; bile leaking from the corner of his mouth. She hadn't meant to kill him, it was an accident. Nothing more than a tragic accident. It sounds trivial, doesn't it? Insignificant? But it was not. Her face twisted with pain. Rather like the domino effect, one event – a fatal accident – initiated a succession of events; a cumulative effect, like ripples on the surface of the water. Actions have consequences.

Chapter 1

She listened. The sound of silence rang in her ears. Inhaling the fresh air deep into her lungs, she breathed in her first salty taste of freedom. She had fled the shores of England as a fugitive, a missing person, and now, at last, she had arrived. She exhaled, watching as her breath condensed in the cold air. Perhaps her memories would fade in time, like her breath. But, for now, she must block them out and focus on the future. Her name is Céline Dupont. Her mother was French and she had been brought up to be bilingual.

Gazing out towards the land, a familiar nervous fluttering rose from deep in the pit of her stomach; there was no time to lose. But first she must do something important. She hurriedly scribbled an unsigned note to the owners of the yacht, apologising for the theft, and folded the note around a wodge of cash, to reimburse them for relocation expenses and any inconvenience caused. Her conscience was appeased; in part, anyway. Now she must work quickly. The harbour master might appear any minute or, worse still, the French Customs might come aboard and want to see the vessel's paperwork. She opened the locker and pulled out an inflatable dinghy, rolled up neatly, and a pump. Dragging the heavy package up onto the deck, she unrolled it, and plugged in the foot pump, heaving with exertion as the air gradually filled the tubes of the dinghy. Before long, it was fully inflated and she could slide it over into the silvery stream of water that was ebbing quite strongly towards the sea. She secured it to the stern, next to the boarding ladder, which had been so useful in the River Dart. She returned to the locker and found two wooden oars. She must gather anything that might be useful from the boat, including her rucksack, containing cash and the gold. Searching in the chart table, she found a small roll of euros; the boat had obviously made the crossing to the coast of France before. She rummaged in the side lockers in the cabin and selected a rain sou'wester, a pair of sunglasses and a woolly scarf. She knew that it would be important to blend in with the locals.

As Céline pulled away from the yacht, she caught sight of the name of the boat – *La Mouette* – and realised that, quite by chance, she had chosen a boat with a French name. Perhaps this was a good omen. Her uncle, a yachtsman, had told her many years before, that sailors have always been very superstitious: they would never set off on a voyage on a Friday, or whistle on board, in case they whistled up the wind and brought on a storm.

Everything seemed so difficult. She felt gnawing hunger in her belly, having not eaten for hours. She threw her meagre possessions into the dinghy and clambered in. Her chest heaved with the weight of the oars, as she battled against the strong tide, but it was taking her seaward, rather than to the landing stage, which she could see near the village. She pulled with all her might, realising that she should have aimed upstream of her desired landing point.

Eventually, struggling to catch her breath, Céline headed towards a sandy cove just beyond a small promontory. The current slackened and she could finally make her way towards the beach, sheltered from the mainstream. She pulled the dinghy up the sand and secured the painter onto the root of a tree, that seemed to be made just for this purpose. She gave a deep sigh and wondered why on earth people do this kind of thing for pleasure. As her feet sunk in the wet sand and seaweed, her cracked lips formed a smile. She had made it. It crossed her mind that this is what it must have been like for women who were dropped in France to liaise with the French resistance in the Second World War. But at least they had paperwork, she did not.

She must head for the nearest train station; but first, she must find a café to have some much-needed sustenance. Her whole body ached and she felt as if she hadn't slept for a week. She made her way up the beach and onto the narrow coastal road, and, after a short walk, opened the door to a small café and inhaled the evocative aroma of coffee. Finding a table near the window, she ordered a *café au lait* and a plate piled high with pastries, feeling pleasantly surprised that the elderly gentleman who served her understood her rather hesitant French, without correcting her. Perhaps her use of language wasn't too bad.

Staring out of the window, she could just see the distant blue line where the sea separated the land from the sky.

She felt quietly satisfied that she had made the first part of her journey unscathed. The Channel crossing had gone relatively smoothly, and she had successfully anchored in the Rance estuary, close to Dinard, a small town a few kilometres from Saint Malo. So far, so good. Her sketchy plan was to catch a train down south to Marseille. She had discovered on the internet that it was becoming easier and easier for illegal immigrants to get their hands on fake ID cards in France. Many of the bogus documents had fooled the police, and, if she could organise this, she could then look for a job. It would be risky and expensive, but she had no choice.

Céline lingered, clutching the cold mug to her chest. How had it come to this? Her eyes glazed over with the memories: her chaotic life in Oxford; her marriage to Alex; of the bullying, the put-downs, and of being constantly undermined. She had been coercively controlled by her husband and she had obeyed. She had truly believed his cruel words. But all for what?

Her thoughts were interrupted by the elderly gentleman, gazing at her with concern. '*Plus de café?*'

Céline was surprised how easily her French flowed. She declined another coffee, and asked directions to the local train station. As she got up to leave, the gentleman smiled softly, grasping her hand in his. '*Bon courage, madame.*'

As the train pulled away from the platform, she gazed out of the window, watching as the flat countryside of Northern France sped by. Everything was on a larger scale: the farmland fields, defined by low-level walls or bushes, were huge, twice the size of the fields she had grown to love in Devon. Her mind returned to Loss, a small coastal town near Dartmouth, where she had fled, following tragic events in Oxford. She screwed her eyes tightly against the harsh reality. But she had found some happiness in Loss, working as a live-in nanny for two young children. She remembered the friendships she had made; close friends, both in Oxford and in Loss. Real friendships were hard to come by, and she had been forced to leave them all behind. Uncurling the fingers of one hand, she counted them one at a time: five fingers, five friends. Four strong inspirational women, and one very special man. She had heard it said that, in life, you can usually count true friends on the fingers of one hand. For her, it was true.

But one of those friends lingered longer in her mind: Sandy, a brilliant musician, who she had met during her time in Loss. Sandy had survived a tough childhood: she had overcome prejudice, and her disability, and had emerged as a strong woman who inspired and who shone. Sandy had taught her that everything is possible, if you keep your mind open to all the exciting opportunities in life. She had grown to love Sandy, and promised herself that they would meet up again one day. But, for now, she strengthened her resolve to be strong, remain focussed, and keep her mind open to the limitless possibilities that her future would present to her. She would draw strength and inspiration from Sandy, a wonderful and significant friend.

The clouds scudded across the enormous expanse of deep-blue sky. Her mind wandered to her weekend in

Paris two years before. She had been struck then by the ceiling-less French skies, so very different from the low skies of England, but perhaps this was just an illusion. She thought about the unique experiences she had enjoyed at an exclusive libertine club in a redundant château. She had learnt a huge amount about herself; about her own sensuality and sexuality; about the importance of showing respect for herself and for others; and for the significance of loving, open and honest relationships.

Before she fled from England, she completed her memoir, *The Humble Pawn*, writing under a pseudonym, Antonia Farouk. Pulling no punches, she had included the unabridged horror of her life and details of the shocking tragedy. The manuscript had been accepted for publication. Probably nothing would come of it, but she couldn't help but wonder.

So how did it happen? Why did it happen? Céline waited for the inevitable agony of the past to engulf her, like a thick impenetrable fog.

Chapter 2

She woke up with a jolt as the train screeched to a standstill at Gare de Marseille-Saint-Charles. The platform was bustling with people all going about their daily business. Overwhelmed, Céline waited until the carriage was nearly empty of passengers, collecting her thoughts for the next stage of her journey. Her number-one priority was to obtain a false ID card. She knew this would be challenging; she had no documentation whatsoever. Her second priority was to find a job, preferably a live-in role, so that she wouldn't have the additional worry of finding accommodation. And one where she could work for "cash in hand" because she didn't have a bank account.

The opulent station perched on a small hill, with a grand set of stairs linking it to the city. It felt light and airy and, as she stepped out onto a large open terrace, sweeping views of the city of Marseille stretched out before her. On the left she could see the impressive outline of *La Basilique Notre-Dame de la Garde*, a Catholic basilica situated high on a hilltop, just south of *le Vieux Port*, the Old Port. How she longed to be a tourist, with enough time to explore this splendid city; she would love to visit some of the restaurants famous for local seafood or visit the infamous *Château d'If* on its own island out in the bay, France's very own seventeenth-century Alcatraz, but she must press on.

She turned back into the station area and gazed at the sign leading to fourteen dead-end platforms. How would she ever find her way out of this impressive station? Passing a kiosk, she bought a coffee and a chocolate bar. It felt comforting to find her favourite treat, even in a different country. She knew that, before too long, she must have a proper meal to fortify herself for whatever lay ahead.

Her gut instinct told her that she should head for the poorest, crime-ridden part of Marseille. She'd read that northern districts of the city were corrupt, dangerous and brutal to the poor, in stark contrast to the gleaming white monolithic buildings and richness found in the southern area of Marseille. The boundary is defined by the sea and by mountains, so the poorer districts are all located within the city boundary.

She would head for *les quartiers nord de Marseille* – the northern quarter – where, in some areas, over fifty per cent of the population live well below the poverty line. She would have to take care, but here, she would be more likely to obtain the documentation she needed.

Noticing a neon sign advertising safe storage, she knew it would be advisable to store a large amount of cash, jewellery and gold in a safe deposit box in the station building. It would be dangerous to wander around the northern quarter with all her worldly goods in a rucksack. This was remarkably easy to organise and, relieved, she packed sufficient euros in her money belt to see her through the next few days.

At last, she had walked the interconnecting stairs to the centre and decided to head for the Old Port and find a hotel for the night, before heading to the north of the city the next day. It was a short walk – less than two kilometres – and as she approached the lively marina, she was struck by the huge variety of boats, both old and new, and the colourful facades of the local seafood bars and restaurants. She strolled along the quay, breathing in the vibrant atmosphere. No wonder the Old Port is often described as the beating heart of France. The sea breeze brushed her face, and she could almost forget her circumstances and enjoy the pleasures of this beautiful district of Marseille.

Selecting a small waterside bistro, she sat on one of the tables just inside the bar, overlooking the swaying masts in the marina. She ordered *un plateau de fruits de mer* – a plate of seafood – and half a litre of *Picpoul de Pinet*, an aromatic wine made in the Languedoc-Roussillon region. She sighed, determined to enjoy a rare moment in the South of France. The variety of shellfish, served on a three-tier platter, was impressive: oysters, crab, mussels, prawns, whelks, clams and other molluscs, all beautifully displayed on ice, and served with a generous portion of French bread, half a lemon, and some mayonnaise. The wine was cool, light and refreshing. She savoured every delicious morsel.

'*J'adore les coquillages*,' said a stylishly dressed young woman, licking her lips seductively. 'You have made a very good choice.'

Céline jumped; she had got used to her own company, and was not expecting to engage in any conversation, not least with the chic French women sitting on the table beside her. The stranger fondled her golden cashmere scarf between her well-manicured fingernails. *'Bonjour, je m'appelle Nicole. Enchantée,'* she said, reaching over to shake Céline's hand.

'Moi c'est Céline.'

Her new-found acquaintance exuberantly pushed her chair back and leant over to kiss her lightly on both cheeks. 'May I join you?' Without waiting for an answer, Nicole dragged her chair across to share the table. Céline made a mental note to stay on her guard, and not reveal anything about her past. But she had immediately warmed to this woman, and she welcomed the chance to practise her French and have some friendly conversation.

Nicole had attractive features and well-defined cheekbones. Her long sun-bleached hair was drawn back in a messy bun, revealing eye-catching diamond stud earrings. She wore a loose-fitting beige jumpsuit in sheer fabric, and a diamond-encrusted gold Rolex around her bronzed wrist. She looked elegant and sophisticated, and seemed friendly and approachable. 'This is my favourite bistro, I always meet interesting people here. It is simple and unassuming from the outside, so I find that only the most discerning people choose to dine here, rather than the more expensive and touristy restaurants at the other end of the harbour,' she said, screwing up her nose and pointing dismissively to a group of buildings further up the curved promenade. They all looked very inviting but had no customers.

'I always choose a restaurant based on how popular it is,' Céline offered. 'Look, it's already filling up with people, and it isn't even lunchtime yet.' She began to relax as she sipped the chilled wine.

'You are right.' Nicole sighed extravagantly. 'It is a very pleasant way to pass the time of day. I'm often on my own here. My husband is away on business, *again*. I wouldn't be at all surprised if he is with another woman, he often is…'

'Really?'

'Yes, but it is fine with me, he can do as he pleases.'

'But doesn't this make you sad? Or angry?' Céline blurted out. She could hardly believe that, within five minutes of conversation, Nicole was already opening up to her about intimate details of her married life.

'It doesn't worry me at all,' she purred. 'He always comes back to me in the end.' She laughed. 'I'm like an old and comfortable settee! Do you know what I mean? We are good together. And, if I meet someone, then I know he would feel the same…'

'You are certainly unlike any old comfortable settee I've ever seen, but I do understand what you mean. You feel safe and secure enough in your relationship to allow each other space and freedom.' Céline stared into the distance. The sentiments Nicole had expressed reminded her of a good friend, Roland, who held similar moral beliefs.

'Exactly. If Jacques – my husband – is enjoying himself with another woman when he is away, then he always comes home happier and more content. I think he realises that the grass isn't always greener on the other side.' She paused. 'How are the shellfish? Oysters are my favourite, but I also love *les bulots* – very tasty sea snails. Some people find them rubbery and chewy, but that is only because they choose the big ones, the smallest ones are always the best. Now, I've told you a little about myself, what about you? Are you planning to be in Marseille for long?'

Céline's face reddened. 'There isn't much to say really. I'm not sure where I'm heading, but I must find a job before too long to earn some money.'

'Zere is somezing about your accent...' Nicole drawled, in a low heavily accented voice. 'I zink you are not from France. You are from England? Yesss?' Her plump lips moved seductively to form the words that she spoke. 'Am I... er... right?' she asked, raising her eyebrows. 'My English... it is not zat gooud!'

Céline smiled, acknowledging Nicole's attempt to speak English, but then drew breath. She had been pleasantly surprised that she had understood most of the French conversation and been able to converse fluently, but now she began to feel less confident. How much could she tell Nicole without jeopardising her future? 'My mother came from France and, although I was brought up in England, we spoke a lot of French. My parents are both dead now, but I am keen to return to where she lived as a child to find out more about my ancestry.'

'This sounds very interesting. Where was your mother born?'

'She was born and brought up in the Languedoc region, which I think is now called Occitanie. They lived in a small fishing village called Marseillan on the banks of the Étang *de Thau*. Have you ever been there?'

'We went there a couple of years ago. They make some fine wines in that part of France. And, of course, the area is famous for Noilly Prat, a white wine vermouth, it's a delicious aperitif.'

'My goodness, I would love to know more about how wine is produced. It must be a hard life working in a vineyard,' she said, raising her glass to her lips.

'We have friends who own a vineyard in Occitanie, and you are right, it is a tough existence. Pascal and Sophia, the owners of Château Pascal, devote their whole lives to the fruit on the vine, working tirelessly day in, day out. They can't even leave the vineyard to go on holiday, or even to visit friends,' she said wistfully. 'They are a unique couple. But sadly, we hardly ever see them.'

'Perhaps I could visit them to see how the grapes are made into wine,' Céline said, her eyes shining. 'It is something that has interested me for a long time, and the vineyard is in the area of France that I intend to visit.' She cleared her throat. 'That is, if they're not too busy.'

Nicole gazed at Céline thoughtfully. 'I'm sure they would welcome you.'

'*Voila, madame*,' the waiter said, placing the first part of her order of broth with slices of toasted French bread rubbed with garlic and topped with *rouille* – a rich sauce made with egg yolk, chilli powder and olive oil. '*Merci*, Sébastien,' Nicole said, acknowledging the waiter. '*Bouillabaisse* is a famous Provençal delicacy.' She paused to sample the broth. 'It is perfect, and this is only the start.

You wait until you see the fish and potatoes that he will bring out in a minute.' She licked her lips in anticipation.

Céline was beginning to wish that they were sitting on a larger table, this was becoming a culinary feast requiring lots of serving dishes. Soon the waiter arrived with an impressive platter of fish: bass, red mullet, and halibut, with mussels and squid. 'The fisherman brought in a fine catch this morning,' he commented with a smile. An earthenware pot of steaming potatoes was placed beside the fish.

'It looks absolutely delicious.'

'It is the saffron and the spices that make the dish special. And the fish has to be firm and fresh. I always know when I order this dish, that these beauties were alive and well, and swimming in the Mediterranean only yesterday.' She pointed to Céline's rapidly diminishing plate of seafood. 'I do love *les coquillages* but there is nothing like *bouillabaisse*, especially when it is made locally in Marseille.'

Céline smiled. It was refreshing to see someone overtly enjoying food, and she wondered idly how Nicole kept her slim figure.

'I'm staying in our waterside apartment just a few minutes' walk from here, would you like to come to my place for an espresso? I have a machine that makes excellent coffee.'

Using a fine utensil to pull out the flesh of her final *bulot*, Céline wondered if it would be wise to accept the invitation but consoled herself with the fact that she had little to lose, and everything to gain. 'That would be great, Nicole, thank you.'

Waving her gold credit card in front of the waiter, Nicole insisted on paying. '*Avec plaisir!*'

The door opened and the two women stepped into the light, spacious apartment. The sun streamed in through the ceiling-to-floor glass windows, overlooking the port. The outside world seemed to be a natural extension of the inside, with magnificent views of the Old Port, the bay, and of *Château d'If*, rising majestically out of the shimmering blue water. Céline absorbed the vista, struck by the sheer beauty of the harbourside and of the serenity and style of the decor inside the apartment. The luxurious blue damask sofas were low level, chic and adorned with a collection of yellow and navy scatter cushions. The natural ceramic, tiled floor and vociferous indoor plants gave a Mediterranean atmosphere, reminding Céline of a hot summer's day. She opened the glass door to the balcony and sat on one of two patio chairs. It felt surreal to be in an elegant Mediterranean apartment, having sailed from Dartmouth a couple of days before. She had left one country as Charlie and arrived on the shores of France as Céline. She felt a tiny flutter of optimism. Perhaps she could, at last, leave her past life truly behind her and start all over again.

Chapter 3

'It's a crazy idea to go and search for a hotel tonight. We have a spare bedroom, you can stay here with me.'

'How kind, Nicole, it is very tempting to…'

'Great. Let's have another glass of wine. What are your plans for tomorrow?'

'Well…' Céline paused. 'I'm planning to go to the northern quarter of Marseille.'

'*Mon Dieu.* What on earth would possess you to go there? It is an area riddled with crime.' She stared at Céline angrily. 'You would be risking your safety.'

'Every city has rough areas, I will be fine.'

'Why on earth would you want to go there when you could wander along the promenade or visit *La Basilique Notre-Dame de la Garde*?'

'I have a problem.' Céline paused, staring dismally out towards the darkening sky of evening. 'I have misplaced my ID card and my passport. I have no other means of identification. Without this, I'm in danger of being deported. I would have no chance of staying in France, or of getting a job.' She tossed her head back defiantly. 'I've done my research, and it would be relatively easy to obtain a false ID card in the northern quarter, but it would cost me a lot of money.'

'Misplaced your ID card and your passport? *Vraiment*?' she said, cocking her head in disbelief.

'I've been very stupid,' Céline muttered.

'Why don't you just go to the authorities and apply for a new one? I'm always losing my ID card.' She pursed her lips and blew out a stream of air. 'And as for your passport, *ooh la la*.'

'It's complicated, I have a lot to sort out at home.'

'Okay, it's really none of my business, but I have a suggestion. There are plenty of people who can forge documents without having to go to the northern quarter.' Nicole walked slowly towards the window, the silence heavy between them. She turned to face Céline. 'I know of a small business that operates just over the border in Spain. The company produces fake ID as a sideline, although, of course, they don't advertise this. They would provide you with the paperwork you need, but I'm afraid it will cost you many euros,' she said, rubbing her thumb and middle finger together. 'The quality will be better than in the backstreets, and much less dangerous for you. In fact, you can do it all by post. You will need to send a photograph with your address, name and date of birth.'

'But I don't have a fixed address at the moment. Could that be a problem?'

'Then make one up,' Nicole said in a loud whisper. 'Perhaps it would be wise to choose a building in multiple occupation where lots of people live in separate rooms. This is simply a business transaction between you and the company... Tomorrow we will organise a photograph and send it with your details, express delivery. It might take a few days, but you can stay here until you have all the paperwork you need.'

'Thank you.' She was relieved that she had been spared the stress of visiting the northern quarter. If only it had been as simple as losing all her documentation. She felt terrible, believing that she was abusing Nicole's trust, but she had no choice. 'But why are you doing all this for me?'

'I think I'm a pretty good judge of character, and I liked you from the moment I met you, and I do so love meeting new people. Have you got enough spare clothes with you?'

'No. I'm travelling light.'

'Then we have to go shopping tomorrow. I know all the best places to shop. I might even treat myself to a couple of new outfits. Oh, I can't wait,' she said, rubbing her hands together gleefully. Céline was glad that she had enough euros with her to buy a few clothes.

At that moment, the front door opened, and in strode a young man. 'Phew, it's hot out there tonight,' he said, planting a kiss on his wife's lips. '*Ooh la la*, you didn't tell me we had a guest,' he said, turning to Céline, and giving *la bise*. 'Nicole never ceases to surprise me,' he said, with a salacious wink. '*Bonjour. J'e m'appelle Jacques. Enchantée.*'

She smiled shyly. '*Moi c'est Céline.* Good to meet you, Jacques. Nicole has kindly suggested that I can stay the night. We met in the bistro, just along the promenade...'

She glanced at Nicole, and thought she saw a flicker of annoyance flash across her face.

'*Mon chéri*, I didn't expect you back for days. I thought you were at a conference until next week.'

'Things didn't quite go according to plan, so here I am. And it means that I am fortunate enough to meet your friend,' he said with a broad smile that lit up his face.

Jacques was unconventionally good-looking with thick salt-and-pepper hair and tanned skin. His sparkling blue eyes shone from behind round tortoiseshell glasses, in a style that was popular in the nineteen fifties. Tall and casually dressed in a light-blue linen suit, he carried himself confidently; he had the body of an athlete. But what caught her eye the most was his mischievous smile and attractively dimpled cheeks. She liked the way he made direct eye contact with her, and didn't look her up and down, like so many men had done in the past. Jacques made her feel totally at ease.

Balancing a large glass of red wine in his hand, he sank heavily into the downy softness of the sofa. 'Well, what are the plans for tomorrow?'

Nicole smiled. 'We have a few errands to run in the morning, and some clothes shopping. And in the afternoon, we'll probably visit one or two of the more impressive tourist attractions. How does that sound, Céline?'

'Sounds good to me.'

'The weather is forecast to be hot and sunny tomorrow,. I can't believe it's autumn, it feels more like midsummer,' Jacques said, peeling off his jacket. 'I think Céline would have a damn sight more fun if we were to explore the city coastline from out in the bay. Why don't we go out on the boat and do some fishing tomorrow afternoon? With any luck and a following wind, we might even catch a bass or a *dorade royale* to pop on the barbecue for supper.'

Memories of the last time she had been on a boat came flooding back. Céline was quietly proud that she had managed to single-handedly navigate *La Mouette* across the Channel and arrive safely on the shores of France. She wondered if she might have some unexpected skills. 'That sounds amazing. I would absolutely love to go fishing!'

Nicole sighed with disappointment. 'I guess we can fit everything in, except the touristy bits, in the morning, and we can always take a picnic lunch onto the boat.' Nicole generally found sailing and fishing rather dull, but the prospect of good company, delicious food and wine, and the promise of blue sky and sunshine made the proposal seem quite attractive.

***

It was like looking down the barrel of a gun. She held her breath and waited for the inevitable. The room filled with a series of white flashes, momentarily blinding her. Then it was done. After what seemed like an eternity, she reached into the dispenser and pulled out a strip of slightly damp photographs.

'They don't look anything like you,' said Nicole, grinning from ear to ear. 'You look like an escaped convict.' She threw back her head and roared with laughter. 'No passport photo I've ever had looks like me! I don't know why they bother. Anyway, the moment you change your hairstyle, or, dare I say it, your face ages, you look even less like the photo they use to identify you. Madness, if you ask me.'

Céline stared at the strip of photos. Her friend was right, none of the images looked anything like her. She sighed with relief. 'They'll do…' She pulled out her Swiss Army Knife from her left pocket and cut the photos up into four separate images. Turning two of them over, she signed and wrote on each one in capital letters: CÉLINE DUPONT: 11/03/1990. Job done. She placed them carefully into an envelope and gave them to Nicole to add further details and send to the company in Spain, express delivery.

After pausing for an espresso, the two women made a lightning tour of a number of exclusive boutiques and selected clothes for the autumn and for the winter months ahead. Nicole had a keen eye for selecting stylish and fashionable clothes, teaming up classic outfits: trousers, skirts and tops, with simple, eye-catching accessories: scarfs, jackets and jewellery. She was also quick to spot a bargain, selecting skimpy summer dresses and sarongs, and one or two bikinis in the summer sale. Struggling under the weight of their purchases, they made their way back to the apartment. After a quick espresso, Nicole slipped back into town to buy a picnic lunch, leaving Céline to try on her wares. She was pleasantly surprised by most of the outfits, which fitted her perfectly and complimented her skin tone and hair. She particularly liked the biscuit-coloured cashmere jumper that enhanced her figure and felt luxuriously soft against her skin. She wondered how on earth all her new clothes could possibly fit into her rucksack, but this was a worry for another day. She was looking forward to the afternoon. The weather forecast had been right: the sky was a deep blue with small oval cigar-shaped clouds, unlike any she had ever seen before. The bay almost seemed to be calling her, shimmering and sparkling in the midday sun.

She selected some navy-blue trousers, a pink cotton shirt and a pair of pumps for the afternoon ahead. Suddenly, Nicole returned, banged the front door, and she blew into her bedroom like a whirlwind. 'What's wrong, Nicole? Are you okay?'

'I can't believe it. My mother is in a care home in Aix-en-Provence, and she has had a fall. *Maman* has asked to see me. I have to go, Céline, I'm sorry.'

'Of course, you must go, Nicole. Your poor mother. Would it make it easier if I find a hotel nearby for the next couple of nights?'

'Absolutely not. Jacques is looking forward to taking you fishing and I'm sure you will enjoy it.' She hurried out of the room and Céline was left with her thoughts. She had only just met Jacques, and she had immediately warmed to him, but would he really want to devote an afternoon to her, a complete stranger? Would it be wise to go alone on a boat with a man she had only just met? She was sorry that Nicole wasn't joining them; would the conversation be rather awkward?

'Jacques has just phoned. He would like to meet you at the marina entrance at one o'clock.' Placing a large hamper at Céline's feet, she smiled. 'It's a huge picnic. It should keep you going for a few hours.' She threw a few things into her suitcase and, pausing by the door, she cupped Céline's hands in hers. 'Jacques will look after you well, Céline, you will be safe with him. Just relax and enjoy a good afternoon out.' With that, she kissed Céline and left, closing the door behind her. 'À *bientôt*.'

Céline considered all her options carefully, deciding in the end to throw caution to the wind. She looked at her watch. She would have to hurry, she only had ten minutes before she was due to meet Jacques. She hurriedly drew a brush through her hair and grabbed the spare key to the apartment. Taking a deep breath, she resolved to enjoy an invitation to go cruising on a hot afternoon, with a friendly skipper in the Mediterranean.

'*Salut*, Céline,' he said, brushing his lips on both her cheeks. '*Il fait très chaud cet après-midi*. It's just as well you're not doing the tourist trails this afternoon, it would have been unbearably humid. It will be lovely out in the bay, we'll have a cooling breeze off the water. Nicole is going to miss a treat, but actually, she doesn't seem to enjoy cruising as much as she used to.' He stared out towards the horizon. 'When we first bought our boat, we used to have great times together exploring the coastline,' he said wistfully. 'But I'm sure she would rather be with us than travelling in a stuffy car to see *Maman*.' He cradled Céline's arm in his and together they walked along the pontoon until they approached a gleaming blue-hulled thirty-five-foot motor yacht. 'Welcome to *Carpe Diem*,' he said, as he helped her aboard.

'*Carpe Diem*, I think it comes from Roman times. It means *live for today*.'

'Exactly, Céline. We must seize the moment. Yesterday has gone, and tomorrow might never happen. We must grab the rich opportunities life has to offer, because we're a long time dead.'

His words cast a shadow as Céline's thoughts returned to her husband, Alex, and his untimely death. She must try to put the past behind her and live in the moment. Her face broke into a smile. 'And I am grabbing this amazing opportunity. I didn't expect to be cruising the Med today.'

'*Bienvenue dans mon paradis.*'

Chapter 4

'Let's put all our worries aside and enjoy the afternoon to the fullest.'

Céline bit her lip; it was as if Jacques had read her mind.

'I'll show you around, and then we must get cracking.' Down below, the living area was spacious. The galley was narrow but well equipped with a fridge, gas cooker and hob, sink and draining board, and ample storage space. 'The only thing the galley doesn't have is a dishwasher!' He chortled. 'Nicole designed most of the interior decor of the boat, and she insists on good quality and coordinated colours.'

Opposite the galley was the chart table, with a plethora of instruments and screens, that Céline thought might have been useful on her cross-Channel trip, had she known how to use them. 'Here are the heads, the bathroom to you landlubbers. You must remember not to put anything down the loo that hasn't already been eaten. It's very simple to use: just put down the lid, press the button, and the waste is pumped into a holding tank. There are a couple of sleeping cabins: the master cabin, and the guest cabin in the stern. The boat holds four people comfortably.'

A varnished folding table separated two luxurious seating areas in the saloon. The curtains, framing the long narrow portholes, had a cheery blue-and-white nautical theme, reflected in the scatter cushions. A clock and barometer were displayed on one side of the bulkhead, and on the other side there was a framed painting of *Carpe Diem* planing across the bay at full speed, the French tricolour proudly streaming astern, and set against a backdrop of Marseille.

'Right, let's get moving. I'll start the engines and make a few checks. Make yourself comfortable up on the bridge.' She climbed up and studied the deck; it felt like a huge white plastic toy, with a lot of gadgets: instruments, levers, screens and buttons. It was nothing like the boat she had last travelled on. She was relieved that she could relax this afternoon with no responsibility.

The air suddenly filled with the sound of the engines firing up, a thick white cloud of smoke, and the noxious smell of diesel exhaust fumes. He let the engines run while he made various checks, including fuel and water levels. He had already contacted the marina staff to help him with his warps, as he was essentially a single-handed sailor, and before long they were heading out towards the open sea.

Her chest heaved with a mixture of excitement and trepidation. The bay was alive with all kinds of boats – large and small, motorboats and yachts – all out enjoying the unseasonably warm weather and calm sea. She felt grateful that she didn't have to negotiate the boat through the frenetic tangle of activity in front of them.

Jacques sat on the helmsman's seat behind the large circular steering wheel, steadfastly steering a path to the right of the bay. He looked totally at ease and unperturbed by the chaotic scene unfolding in front of him. At last they reached the mouth of the bay and headed out into the open sea. Céline watched as the boat cut a white ribbon through the deep clear water. As the speed increased, the bow rose, and the lumpiness of before turned to calm. It reminded Céline of her riding days, the difference between trotting and galloping. She closed her eyes, revelling in the warmth of the sun and the soft feel of the breeze as it caressed her cheeks.

All of a sudden, Jacques turned the wheel and a small rocky cove opened up before them. There were a couple of boats already anchored to one side, so Jacques headed for the quieter, more secluded end of the cove. 'This is usually a great place to pick up a few bass, but I fear the water is too clear today and the fish will be wary of us. Usually, I like to go *catching* rather than go fishing, but today, I'll put out the fishing lines and we'll see what happens.' He slowed the engines down to a stop, pressed a button, and the anchor began to drop, making a rhythmical clunking sound as the chain passed round the electric windlass.

Finally peace descended. Céline hadn't appreciated quite how intrusive the sounds were until the engines were cut. All she could hear was the water gently lapping against the hull, and the distant hum of a group of youngsters chatting and laughing on one of the boats in the distance. 'It's amazing how sound carries over water, isn't it?'

'It's true. I often wonder why there aren't more music festivals based on cruise ships performing to an audience on land. The quality of sound would be amazing, and they could entertain vast crowds of people.'

'Great idea. Perhaps you should suggest this to the Mayor of Marseille.'

'Huh, I don't think our mayor has a creative bone in her body. She's a crusty old soul with no sense of humour. But maybe you're right, I should have a chat with her. I'll take a bottle of my finest whisky with me; so many French people love to collect single malts. I think it may help my cause.'

Céline smiled at the thought of bribing the mayor. 'Do you ever come across any dolphins?'

'I can call dolphins to the boat by thumping on the side of the hull. They can't resist coming to find out what's going on.' His eyes sparkled with pleasure. 'I adore dolphins, they are such fun and always lift my spirits. They're such mischievous creatures, always ducking and diving in the waves, with wide smiles on their faces. I like to hear them whistle and click... They remind me of our town council meetings, where everyone has a strong view, and some think that, by shouting louder, they're more likely to get their point across.' He laughed. 'They do a lot of tail and flipper slapping, bumping into each other, and spy hopping.'

'Who? The counsellors or the dolphins?'

'Haha, very funny.' They both laughed.

'Spy hopping sounds intriguing. What does it mean?'

'Dolphins are curious creatures, and when they want to see what's going on above the surface, they rise vertically out of the water to have a look. They're so clever. And did you know that dolphins make sounds under the water that can be heard by other dolphins, up to twenty kilometres away? Isn't that incredible.'

Céline raised her eyebrows in surprise.

'And I'll tell you another fascinating fact. Dolphins have sex for fun, not simply for procreation. They have the right idea! They're more like humans than we might think,' he said with a wide grin. 'It's a great philosophy, isn't it?'

'Wow, who'd have believed it?' she said, playfully dismissing his question. 'How do you know so much about sea life, Jacques?'

'The sea is in my soul. I've been a sailor all my life. I come from a family of fishermen, but I diverged into something more profitable. I could see that there was no future for small fishing businesses, and sadly the Mediterranean has been overfished; people are too greedy. So now, fishing is my hobby, and banking is my profession. Banks will always be needed. I know we're despised by parts of society, but when people need a loan for their business, or a house, what would they do without us?'

'Good point, Jacques. We don't all have the backing of family money. I'm an educator, and I've often thought that we need to put more emphasis on the teaching of life skills, like organising finances and managing a household budget. All subjects are, of course, valid and important, but unfortunately there isn't enough time to cover everything... It seems to be all about flashing the credit card these days and picking up the pieces later.'

Jacques stepped down below and returned carrying two fishing rods and a box of bait. 'We'll put these out on the off-chance. I don't hold out much hope today, but you never know, we might be lucky.' He hooked a frozen sand eel onto one of the rigs, and a peeler crab onto the other, and then he cast them gently astern, placing the butts of the rods into the rod holders. Céline admired his confidence. To her, it looked like a tangle waiting to happen. The sleek black rods gleamed in the sunshine, and the golden reels glittered. 'Shall we go to the foredeck and relax on the lounging mattresses for a while before we have our picnic?'

Céline sighed with pleasure. 'Sounds like heaven to me.' As she stretched out luxuriously on the cushions, she could sense a rare feeling of true happiness bubble up from deep within her. The sun beat down on her face and soon she could feel tiny beads of perspiration appear above her top lip. 'Wow, there is a lot of power in the sun, isn't there? I felt deliciously cool when we were speeding on the water, but now…'

Jacques slowly rose to standing, casting a shadow over her body. '*Oui, j'ai trop chaud.* I fancy a dip. I sometimes swim a few times round the boat.'

'Oh that sounds like a good plan.'

'Are you a competent swimmer, Céline?'

'Yes, I learnt to swim when I was four years old and swam a mile when I was seven. I love swimming.'

'I think I'll tie a fender on the stern, just in case the current kicks in,' he said, glancing over the side of the guard wire. 'The water is crystal clear, it looks very inviting, but conditions can change quite quickly. After our swim we must put on some factor-thirty sun cream, we could easily burn today. Will you remind me?'

Céline returned her gaze to the turquoise water that merged into emerald green close to the rocky shoreline. She longed to immerse herself in the cool crystalline water, but she winced internally. She had forgotten to bring her bikini. How could she have left her newly acquired swimwear behind?

Jacques smiled. 'When I swim from the boat, I don't bother with my trunks. Is that okay with you?'

'Of course,' she replied. 'Are you a naturist?'

Jacques looked at her in surprise. 'Are you?'

'I was introduced to naturism a few years ago,' she said, thinking back to her experiences in Paris, where she had swum in a pool in a naturist campsite. And after that in Pilchard Cove in Dartmouth. 'Naturism is a great way to enjoy the elements – the wind, rain and the sun – on your body. It's as simple as that. I remember a friend of mine making me laugh by saying that it was a daft idea to put *on* clothes to go swimming.'

'We have been naturists for years. It is the best way to enjoy swimming, and sunbathing.'

She glanced sideways as he peeled off his navy shorts. His legs were muscular and tanned, his buttocks firm and toned. He lifted his shirt over his head, to reveal an athletic physique, and not a tan line in sight. Céline could feel a small tingle of excitement as she watched him climb over the rail, perform a half pike, and enter the water with hardly a splash. He squinted upwards in the sunlight. 'It's perfect, Céline. In you come.'

Her mind was full of jumbled thoughts. She loved the whole idea of naturism, and it brought back some pleasurable memories of freedom and friendship, but she was still haunted by poor body image. But then she recalled her friends telling her that she had a perfect body. 'I can do this.' She stripped off her flimsy summer dress and underwear, balanced on the teak toe rail of the boat, lifted her arms high, took a deep breath and plunged into the cool glassy water, feeling it ripple deliciously across her body.

'*Ooh la la*, you are amazing.' He placed a wet hand over his mouth, his eyes dancing with mirth. 'I mean, your dive was truly amazing!' He laughed. She felt her inhibitions vanish as they swam together under the dark shadow of the hull of *Carpe Diem*, spluttering as they rose to the surface on the other side of the boat. Enjoying the sensation of weightlessness and freedom, as the water gently caressed her skin, she followed Jacques as he swam towards a small cave carved in the rock. He paused at the entrance, glancing back at Céline, before swimming into the gloom. The air in the cave was dank and heavy: silent, except for a single drip of water that fell rhythmically from the ceiling. 'Isn't this exciting, Céline? It reminds me of the adventure stories I loved to read when I was a child.' His deep voice resonated around the interior walls of the cave. 'Can you imagine how exciting it would be to discover some treasure, or a message in a bottle?'

Smiling, Céline swam near the edge of the cave, exploring all the cracks and crevices. Tiny mussels clung to the rocks, sculpting the uneven surface and shining in the semi-darkness. She gave a shiver, suddenly feeling rather uneasy about what might be lurking beneath the dark water. 'I'm heading back out, I'm getting rather chilly here.'

'Okay, I'm just coming.' Jacques lingered a while longer before emerging into the sunshine, and together they swam to the stern ladder and climbed back on board. They rinsed themselves under the deck shower and dried off with a white fluffy towel. 'Let's go and relax and warm up, Céline. We mustn't forget the sunscreen.' With that, he grabbed the bottle from the cockpit locker and sprayed her all over. She squealed with delight as the strong jet of perfumed lotion splashed against her skin.

Once again, they languished on the deep loungers on the foredeck.

All of a sudden, Jacques turned towards Céline and propped his head on his hand. 'I want to ask you something. It is quite personal, I hope you don't mind.'

Chapter 5

Despite the searing heat, a shiver ran up her spine, and the familiar feeling of dread suffused her once more. She must be on her guard. Keep vigilant. She must not tell.

'Are you in trouble, Céline? Nicole tells me you have lost your passport, and that you have no fixed address. Are you running away from something... or someone?'

She averted her eyes. 'I've done a few things in my past that I'm not proud of...'

'Haven't we all!' Jacques affirmed quietly.

'And I suppose I am running away to find a better life. You know how it is, life isn't always a bed of roses.'

'Or "a bowl of cherries" as I think you English say.' His nut-brown face broke into a smile. 'We can't change the course of history; what's done is done. You must put whatever it is behind you, and it can't be that bad because you're not incarcerated in some grim prison somewhere, or held to ransom by a jealous lover are you?' he proffered.

She drew breath, shocked that he could be so close to the truth about the likelihood of her imprisonment if she was ever to be found. 'It is easier said than done,' she said sadly. 'My world might eventually come crashing down around me. But until that time comes, I'm determined to live more in the moment, like you suggest. We all spend far too much time worrying about the future instead of enjoying ourselves. We can only do our best.'

He gazed at her with overt affection. 'I haven't known you for a long time, Céline, but, to me, you are beautiful, a rare breed, you radiate warmth and kindness.' He paused, looking into her steely blue eyes. 'And I can see that you are fiercely determined. Seize the moment and you will find happiness, I'm sure of it.' He drew his curved fingers lightly down her bare arm, sending tingles of excitement in their wake. 'You're gorgeous,' he whispered in her ear. He placed gentle kisses along her shoulder, continuing down her stomach, brushing her breasts; his lips paying full attention to every part of her body. She snaked her arm around his shoulder and pulled him gently towards her. Her heart was pounding in her ribcage, her whole body buzzing with anticipation and excitement. Maybe it was the atmosphere or the sea air, but she hadn't felt like this for a long time. His fingers lightly walked down towards her inner thigh, and she involuntarily opened her legs as he began to explore her more sensitive areas. She could feel his manhood pressing hard against her thigh. Her whole body was pulsating with pleasure, she heard ringing in her ears.

Suddenly, Jacques sprang to his feet. 'We've caught a fish!'

She looked at him in astonishment.

'Can you hear the bell ringing on the end of the rod? That means there's activity on the end of the line.' He dashed to the stern, leaving Céline feeling deflated. That was the sound she could hear in her ears, nothing to do with passion and excitement.

'Come on, take the rod.'

'What do you want me to do with it? I've never done this before.'

The rod bent as the fish fought strongly. 'Just hold it, I'll get the net.' Céline struggled as the butt dug painfully into her stomach. Jacques took over and played the fish until the line slackened and the fish tired, and he could draw it across the surface and slip the landing net under it.

'What a beautiful specimen, it's like a bar of silver!'

She glanced from the squirming fish to Jacques. He looked elated. 'I really didn't think it was the right conditions to have a bite today, but just look what we've managed to land!'

'It's a big one all right,' said Céline, now focussing fully on the plump fish still quivering in the net.

'I'll just put it out of its misery, and then we should have our picnic. Dreaming about how delicious the bass will taste from the barbecue is making me hungry.' He looked at his watch. 'It's just after four-thirty, no wonder my tummy's rumbling. I've been rather distracted.'

Céline smiled as she felt a wave of relief wash over her. She had enjoyed some warm human contact, and had been excited by his touch, but it was probably just as well that they had been interrupted, though she also felt a deep pang of disappointment. Her last sexual encounter had been with a beautiful musician, a woman. And now she had been sexually excited by a man. She realised that she felt more confident about herself and her body now, more so now than she had ever done before; she was ready to go with the flow and to take any opportunities that were offered to her. After all, you usually only regret the things you don't do in life.

'Come on, let's go and eat.' Jacques went down below and brought up the picnic and a chilled bottle of champagne. He erected the table in the cockpit and spread out an impressive feast of cold hams and salami, pickles and gherkins, olives, pâté and baguette. Large greenish-red tomatoes added colour and, as a finishing touch, he poured a few crinkle-cut crisps into a bowl. 'Nicole has laid on quite a spread for us today.' He carefully opened the champagne and poured the lively bubbles into two crystal glasses. '*Bon appetit!*' he said, as he started to pile food onto his plate. 'I think that is one of the finest bass I have ever caught. I can't believe it took the bait in such clear water. Amazing. Shall we save it until Nicole gets back? She'll be so surprised, and she loves nothing more than a fishy feast.'

She watched as he devoured his food with relish. He really took pleasure in all the good things in life, and he seemed unperturbed by the rude interruption from his amorous advances.

'This ham is delicious, isn't it? It reminds me of the ham we used to eat when I was a child: smoky and tender.'

'You will find that food here is generally very good. I have a few things that I always prioritise in life: sex, *côte de boeuf*, red wine, and fishing. But sex...' His eyes were dancing with pleasure. 'Sex is always at the top of my list.' He glanced at Céline. 'And you, what are your priorities?'

She rubbed her nose thoughtfully. 'I've never really thought about it, but I guess, for me, good health, happiness and friendship have to be my main priorities. After all, without good health, we have nothing. And without happiness and friendship, life wouldn't be as rich.'

'You are right. I enjoy all the good things in life, and I guess I've taken good health as a given.'

'But it isn't a given, is it?' She thought about the dark months in her life when she suffered with the burden of anorexia nervosa. 'These days, a frightening percentage of people have mental health issues and, of course, none of us know if we're going to struggle with a life-threatening illness like cancer.'

He shrugged his shoulders. 'In that case, we should live every day as if it were our last.' He sighed with contentment as he scraped the last morsel of meat from his plate. 'And now, *la fromage*.' He produced five different cheeses – Mimolette, Comté, Brie, Dutch Gouda, and a round of creamy goats' cheese. 'Here, we eat our cheese course with a knife and fork,' he said as he cut a small wedge from each of the cheeses and handed the tempting plate to Céline. 'They all look ripe and ready to eat.'

Céline sampled each cheese. They all had a distinctive flavour, and she thought how much subtle taste can be lost by eating cheese with bread or biscuits. She wiped the corner of her mouth with her index finger. 'I think we are living life to the fullest today, aren't we, Jacques?'

'Not quite but nearly,' he said with a wide grin.

Céline's cheeks reddened. 'What about Nicole?'

'I love Nicole, she is my wife. We are generous within our marriage; we allow each other freedom to explore other physical pleasure but are always open and honest with each other. I will, of course, tell her about the fun we've had this afternoon. I think people take sex too seriously, it's only adults at play, after all.'

Jacques held a gloriously simple view of sex and marriage. For her, it was more complicated and bound up with love and emotion. She wondered if this was because she was looking at sex from a female perspective, but then she thought about one or two of her friends who saw sex as a pleasurable, but not a hugely important, part of life.

'There is a big difference between having sex and making love. The two are equally exciting,' he said, with a wry smile. 'I make love to my wife.'

She gently teased the back of his hand with one finger. His face blossomed radiantly with pure pleasure, revealing the deep dimples at either side of his mouth, and perfect teeth.

'I do understand what you mean by allowing freedom within a partnership to enjoy sex with other people… and the openness and honesty that goes with it. You might be surprised to hear that I went to a libertine club with my then-husband, and some friends. It was a life-changing experience.'

'Wow, I'm impressed. We have many such clubs here in Marseille. If you are here long enough, we could visit one. Did you enjoy some new experiences?'

'I met a lovely French couple – my husband was otherwise occupied – and I was pleasantly surprised by the respectful, safe and light-hearted fun we had together. There was no jealousy at all. My husband even got pleasure from watching me with my new-found friends, and he kissed me affectionately for the first time in months. I learnt such a lot about myself, and I have no regrets. It was one of life's rich experiences, one I will never forget.'

'I love watching Nicole when she is with another man or woman, and we always go home as best of friends.' He gazed at her and grinned.

She stood up, took him firmly by the hand, and led him to the foredeck.

Chapter 6

Everyone crowded into the small kitchen to watch Jacques as he masterfully prepared the fish. 'You are right, Céline, it is a beautiful specimen,' he said proudly, as he added small knobs of butter, a pinch of salt, a few herbs and a generous sprinkling of capers, before wrapping the catch in silver foil and sealing the top to form a pouch, *bar en papillote*. 'I was just telling Nicole about our amazing afternoon on the water.' He sighed with contentment, glancing at Céline before returning his attention to the preparation of the meal. 'Now this little beauty can steam without drying up. My mouth is watering already.'

Céline blushed and looked away. He had obviously been true to his word and told Nicole everything that had happened on the fishing trip. She glanced nervously at Nicole, who was sauntering up to her with a beaming smile. 'You look a little uncomfortable, but there is absolutely no need.' She tutted, throwing an arm extravagantly into the air. 'Guilt is only for those that have done something wrong.' With that, she placed one arm around her waist and kissed her gently on the cheek. Céline inhaled her heady perfume – perhaps Hermès Calèche, she wasn't sure – and started to relax.

Nicole padded onto the balcony. This evening she wore a wrap over a summer dress and leather sandals. Her golden hair was loosely tied back in a ponytail, accentuating her well-defined cheekbones and perfect, unblemished skin. Céline had chosen to wear cut-off jean shorts, a crisp white linen shirt and bare feet. She wondered if she was a little underdressed, but she knew the outfit highlighted her long legs and the healthy glow on her skin from their afternoon at sea.

Jacques appeared at the patio door carrying a bottle of champagne. He balanced it on the table, tipped it on one side, and slowly and with control removed the cork, listening to the slow hiss as the pressure was released. 'Lots of people pop the cork. Madness, if you ask me; most of the bubbles miss the glass altogether. I like to ease the cork out slowly. It should sound like the sigh of a satisfied woman. You know what I mean?' he asked, with a wicked glint in his eye. 'I must get back to the barbecue. Enjoy your oysters.'

Together they sat round the patio table in front of their seafood platter. 'It's a special occasion,' Nicole said, raising her glass. 'We need to celebrate your success.' She winked. 'You and Jacques, you had a mar-vell-ous time, I zink,' she said in broken English. 'I zee the way he looks at you...'

'How is your mother, Nicole?' Céline asked, keen to get on to a less emotive subject.

'*Maman* is just old and a little cantankerous these days. She had a fall – her pride is hurt – but her body is fine, thanks.'

'I dread getting old,' said Céline quietly.

'Don't you think it's strange that most of us hate getting old? We fight tooth and nail against the effect age has on our bodies: the lines, the wrinkles, the saggy bits...' she said, pinching a small roll of skin from her tummy. 'Wrinkles are the rich story of life. Why don't we embrace age in the same way that we do a fine piece of antique furniture, or a tasty morsel of mature cheese?'

'You're right, Nicole. There is a certain *something* that older women have; a kind of physical beauty that transcends the ravages of time. We need to listen more to what the older generation has to say. After all, they have acquired wisdom from the ups and downs of a life well lived.'

They both nodded in agreement. 'Instead, all too often, we seem to want to fold them neatly away in care homes, like *Maman*...' She slumped back in her chair. 'At least I visit her, I suppose. We couldn't accommodate all her needs here, the poor darling.'

'I'm sure you did your best, Nicole, and I bet she loves your visits.'

Nicole's eyes lit up. 'I think she does... and all the other residents. I like to make them all laugh with my silly antics.' Céline studied Nicole. Although she hadn't known her for very long, she was beginning to like her very much. Their conversation was interesting, informative and full of humour and laughter. Céline gazed out beyond the marina to the deep blue of the Mediterranean and wondered why she hadn't explored this part of the world before now. Nicole and Jacques had light in their eyes – *joie de vivre*

– the likes of which she hadn't seen for a while. There didn't seem to be any undercurrents of jealousy and envy that she had often come across in the past. Céline's mind drifted as she lifted a plump oyster to her lips, enjoying the exquisite salty taste of the sea as it slid easily down her throat.

'How are the oysters?' Jacques asked cheerily. 'These ones are from Brittany, they're special because they are flushed through with the clean waters of the Atlantic. We also love the oysters from the Étang *de Thau*. They win a lot of awards. Just as we have different wines or cheeses, it's the same with oysters. Anyway, it's almost time to eat.'

Jacques brought out three plates, a glass bowl brimming with green leaves, and a steaming dish of new potatoes, sprinkled with chopped chives. Finally, he brought the wrapped fish, served on a decorated ceramic plate. He placed it proudly in the middle of the table and smiled. '*Voila*! Ah wait, I have forgotten something.' He went inside, reached into his wine fridge, and brought out a bottle of Montrachet. 'I must tell you about this wine, because it is very special. It is made in Burgundy from Chardonnay grapes, and matured in oak barrels, which helps to give it its wonderful colour and distinctive bouquet. It's a perfect wine to compliment fish.'

'I feel so spoiled. This is a feast fit for a queen,' said Céline.

Jacques proceeded to unwrap the parcel with as much care as if it were a newborn baby. He dished up a generous portion of fish for Céline, taking care not to give her any bones; he understood the anatomy of a fish. She helped herself to a heap of green salad and potatoes and sighed happily with anticipation.

'Now, you must have a pinch of these salt flakes from the Camargue. As they say, the difference between good cooking and great cooking can be as simple as just a little extra salt.'

After they had eaten most of the fish, they relaxed and chatted as they enjoyed the wine.

'It was worth the wait to catch this beautiful fish, wasn't it, Céline? We didn't get bored once. This is the joy of having a good fishing companion, it can become a little tedious on your own,' he said with a salacious wink.

'I took some cheeses out of the fridge earlier, if anyone would like some. I'll go and fetch them,' Nicole said, striding towards the kitchen.

Jacques gazed at Céline, stroking the side of her tanned thigh with his capable hands. 'Well, I hope we can do this again sometime. You are always welcome here. Nicole tells me you are going to Marseillan, a very pretty fishing town. If it doesn't work out, for any reason, do remember, we are here.'

'I will and thank you. I have enjoyed myself more than I thought possible. You and Nicole are very generous.'

After a small nibble of cheese, Jacques produced a bottle Armagnac as a digestif. 'I mustn't drink anymore because I'm meeting a demanding client in the morning, and then I have to entertain her for lunch. I need to keep my wits about me.'

Nicole turned to her phone and selected some slow jazz, which wafted through the apartment from their music streaming system. She turned to Céline. 'We should dance.' The two women moved together as one.

'You've got a good man there, Nicole.'

'There are many good men in Marseille,' she whispered in Céline's ear.

The heat of the day had been overtaken by the cool softness of the evening. The light had dimmed over the majestic masts in the marina, and the crescent moon cast a silvery ribbon over the rippled surface of the Mediterranean. 'Much as I'd love to stay out here for a little longer, I think I'll call it a day,' said Céline quietly. 'It has been perfect, thank you both very much. Can I help with the washing up?' she asked, reluctantly peeling herself away from the tempting curves of Nicole's body.

Nicole giggled. 'That is what we have the dishwasher for. No, you go and have a good night's sleep and we'll see you in the morning. It's going to be another hot day, it feels like the endless summer. Why does that make me think about surfing? Or is it an Indian summer? Anyway, whatever it's called, I love it,' said Nicole, giving Céline another warm embrace. 'À *demain, ma belle.*'

***

She saw his body, bound to the bed; lifeless; his skin pale, almost translucent; bile leaking from the corner of his mouth. But then...

Her eyes widened, unblinking, against the darkness. A shrill scream cut through the night. She pulled her knees tightly to her chest, her skin bathed in a sticky layer of sweat. 'Make it go away.' Tears coursed down her face. She sat bolt upright and stared coldly beyond Nicole into the darkness. Digging her fingernails deeply into her scalp, she winced with pain. But she could not erase the agony of her past.

'Wake up, Céline. You are safe.'

Her body froze. 'Who's there?'

'You've had a nightmare. Breathe deeply, I'm here now.'

Céline drew her body into a tight ball, her ribcage heaving with deep sobs. Nicole waited, gently following the bony promontory of her spine with her index finger. 'I don't know what has happened to you, but it must have been awful. My poor darling.'

Céline held her breath, trying to make sense of what had just happened. Her recurring dreams were terrifying and real; the images always the same, and frighteningly vivid. In the hours of darkness, she was living and reliving her worst nightmare.

Nicole put her arm around her, gently easing Céline's head into the hollow of her shoulder. 'It's just a dream. No one can hurt you now,' she soothed, cradling Céline in her arms as she would a young child. 'Everything will be alright. I promise you, it will.'

Céline, overcome with exhaustion, held somewhere between sleep and wakefulness, relaxed heavily into her arms. 'I'm sorry if I woke you... I sometimes have these nightmares... I...' she stammered.

'Don't give it another thought. Would you like some chamomile tea?'

'Please don't leave me,' Céline implored. 'Please stay with me.'

'*Ma belle.* I'm here, and I'm not going anywhere.'

Chapter 7

As night slowly turned to day, Céline stirred, awoken by troubled thoughts that paced relentlessly round and round in her head. She was worried about how much of her past she had unwittingly disclosed to Nicole in her sleep. How much did she know? She nestled into the soft curves of Nicole's body, drawing comfort and warmth from the close physical contact of another human being. Gazing at Nicole, she wondered if being economical with the truth was as bad as telling lies. Either way, she felt terrible that she had accepted the hospitality, kindness and generosity of this wonderful couple, and she had not been completely honest. She was grateful to have had the privilege of meeting them, but she was consumed with sadness that, all too soon, it would come to an end. It would be hard to leave her new-found friends behind and face the daunting prospect of a future alone once more. But, for today, she was in a safe haven and she would endeavour to push the nightmares into the back of her mind and enjoy every moment of the day ahead.

Easing herself out of bed, she wandered over to the window, opened the blind, and gazed at the watery orange sun as it slowly rose from the navy-blue sea. As she breathed in the serene beauty of early morning, she heard the door open to the entrance of the apartments. A solitary figure closed the front door quietly, and walked with a bounce in his step from the apartments towards the main road leading to the centre of town. Jacques was smartly dressed in a beige linen suit with a white shirt and a floral tie. He held a rather battered, but obviously much-loved, leather briefcase in his hand. As he turned onto the main road, her mind wandered to their day together at sea on *Carpe Diem*. Everything about the day had been perfect: the hot sun and the warm sea, a naked swim, fishing, and some unexpectedly erotic moments. Nicole and Jacques were very open and honest, allowing each other sexual freedom within their marriage, and it seemed to work for them. How lucky they were to have each other.

She glanced around to see Nicole blinking against the light of the morning. 'I'm sorry, I shouldn't have opened the blind. Shall I close it again and you can have another little snooze?'

Nicole stretched out luxuriously on the bed and looked rather like the cat that got the cream. 'I love to feel the warm sun on my face in the morning.' She yawned. 'You're a wonderful sleeping partner, *ma chérie*. I'm usually awake in the grey gloom of dawn with Jacques tossing and turning. It is such a treat to open my eyes to the soft light of day.'

'I'm sorry I woke you up during the night, Nicole.' She shrugged her shoulders. 'You don't want to take any notice of me, I talk a load of nonsense in my sleep.' She raised an eyebrow and turned to Nicole, hoping for reassurance.

'You were muttering something like, "Alex, wake up, please wake up…" I think you were having a terrible nightmare. Who is Alex anyway? One of your old lovers or something?'

Céline blushed. 'Like I said, I talk rubbish sometimes.' She turned away, pursing her lips, determined to end the conversation. She was afraid of what she might give away. 'It looks like another lovely day. What are you up to, Nicole?'

'I'm meeting two of my friends, Marie and Danielle, this morning for coffee. Why don't you come too? We always have a good laugh and a chat.'

'I would love to,' Céline answered, relieved that the awkwardness of the last few minutes had evaporated. 'Is the coffee shop in the town centre?'

'No, it's just a few minutes from here. Let's have breakfast and make a plan for the rest of the day.'

As they ambled towards the café, Nicole raised one hand and waved enthusiastically. '*Coucou!*' Her two friends were already seated at a table overlooking a large tree-lined and cobbled square. The café was already filling up with customers, a hubbub of animated conversation, everyone enjoying a coffee and a chat with friends.

Céline sat quietly, absorbing the atmosphere and the convivial interchanges. She could only catch the gist of the conversation; they were speaking far too quickly for her to fully understand. She cupped her coffee in both hands and enjoyed being a passive observer. Listening to their conversation was rather like listening to a fine symphony: expressive and tuneful, with quieter interludes, rising to a crescendo, everyone talking at once in a wondrous cacophony of sound. She loved everything about the French language.

All of a sudden, all eyes rested on her. 'What brings you to Marseille?'

Céline found herself lost for words. She looked down, shuffling nervously on her chair.

'She is so lucky,' Nicole said, putting a comforting hand on Céline's arm. 'She is as free as a bird to explore this part of the world, and she is keen to study her family history. It sounds fascinating. I dread to think what my ancestors were like…' She threw back her head and laughed, attracting the attention of surrounding customers, especially of a group of young men sitting at a table nearby. 'Perhaps it's safer to let sleeping dogs lie.'

Céline shot a grateful glance at Nicole, who had skilfully defused an awkward situation.

'I love nothing more than curling up with a good book about a family saga that spans many generations. I'm a part-time author, and I hope to write about my own family history one day.' Céline bit her lip, wondering if she had given too much about herself away.

Marie turned to her. 'You write books. How clever. I love to read, but the thought of writing a whole book is frankly too daunting. It must take such a long time, and you lay yourself open to a lot of criticism if people don't enjoy reading your work.'

'That's true, but it is the process of writing that I find cathartic and satisfying.'

'You say you find writing "cathartic". Have you written about something painful that has happened to you in the past?' Marie probed.

Céline rubbed her nose thoughtfully. 'I just find writing a welcome distraction from the inevitable drudgery of everyday life.'

'Well, you've come to the right place,' Danielle interjected. 'I would imagine sitting on the balcony in Nicole's dreamy apartment, overlooking the marina and the Mediterranean, an ideal spot for stimulating your creative juices.'

Céline stared into the distance. How she would love to have a quiet secluded apartment on the south coast of France, with spectacular views, and have the freedom to indulge in what she was really driven to do. To write.

'It's interesting to think about creativity isn't it? What makes one person creative and another person not? What is creativity anyway?' Marie asked, shrugging her shoulders. 'Perhaps it is the ability to think outside the box. To view things from a different angle. To toss all your ideas into the air, play with them, and see where they land.'

'Creativity is a massive concept. You can be creative by doing something as simple as singing in the car or weeding the garden. It doesn't always have to be something big like painting a masterpiece or composing a symphony...' Danielle paused. 'Or writing a book.'

'I used to teach young children, and I believe you can't be truly creative unless you can play. Children can lead the way; they learn everything in their early years through play. Being playful is central to creativity and innovation. We need to free our minds up to the limitless possibilities that life has to offer.'

'You are right, Céline. Playing isn't just for children, we're never too old to be playful,' Nicole said, laughing.

'I think you have a couple of admirers over there, Nici.'

'Are you surprised?'

'I think you suffer from high self-esteem,' Marie said, with a grin. They all laughed.

The rest of the coffee morning passed in a blissful haze of conversation. Céline found that she had gradually begun to tune in to their Southern French dialect and had enjoyed the rich and thought-provoking conversation they had had. One day, she would find an inspirational environment where she could truly unleash her imagination and creativity. One day.

Soon after arriving back in the apartment, the front door bell sounded. Nicole answered the door, talked in a hushed whisper, and signed for a letter. 'Céline, I think this is for you.'

Opening the envelope with great care, she pulled out an ID card with her name, an address, her date of birth, signature, and a small photo of her head and shoulders. It looked authentic and just what she needed. Inside was a brief note from the company, thanking her for her custom.

'This is something you shouldn't take lightly; this will get you through most checks, but it won't stand being technically scrutinised,' Nicole warned. The words sent a cold shiver running up and down Céline's spine.

'I'm glad it has arrived safely.' Taking Céline firmly by

the hand, she led her out to the balcony and invited her to sit down. 'I have some good news. I contacted our friends, you know, the ones from the vineyard in Occitanie, Pascal and Sophia.'

Holding her breath, Céline waited to hear what Nicole had to say.

'They have invited you to spend a few days with them whilst you find your feet and find a job and a place to live.'

Céline smiled. 'That's great, Nicole. Thanks for contacting them.'

'Now I must tell you a little bit more. Pascal is one of the kindest people I know. He would lift heaven and earth to help you. He is also incredibly conscientious, devoting much of his time to the vineyard. He is driven to make Château Pascal a success, a vineyard renowned for producing fine wines. Pascal insists on high standards and he and his team work tirelessly to make this happen. Sophia, on the other hand...' She hesitated. 'I don't really know her at all. She is strikingly beautiful, but it is difficult to know what she is thinking behind her veneer of kindliness. There is just something about her that leaves me unsettled.' She glanced at Céline, her brow furrowed. 'But they do work together well as a team, and I'm sure you will enjoy the experience,' she added reassuringly. 'They can't fail to like you, Céline, and I know that you are keen to visit a vineyard. *Voila!* Here's your chance.'

Céline knew that the time had come for her to go. After the kindness that had been shown to her, she didn't want to outstay her welcome. She must leave by train tomorrow morning.

Chapter 8

The windows rattled in their frames, and heavy sheets of rain battered the glass. Céline lay still, her eyes tightly closed. The cold air seeped into her bones, her skin drenched with sweat, as she tried to rid herself of the terror that consumed her... *His skin pale, translucent; bile leaking from the corner of his mouth.* The nights were always the worst.

The ferocious storm had raged all night. She could faintly hear a gate in the distance as it swung relentlessly on its hinges, the sound almost lost in the ravages of the howling wind. How she wished she could transport herself back to the warmth and comfort of Marseille. She had left yesterday, but it seemed like a lifetime ago. After collecting her belongings from the safe storage at the train station, she had bid farewell to Jacques and Nicole and, with grim determination, she had caught the early morning train bound for Béziers. As her two friends disappeared into the distance, her eyes pooled with tears. She wanted to go home. But she had no home.

Reluctantly, she opened her eyes. The room was sparsely furnished with a dark wood desk and chair to one side, and an embossed ceiling-to-floor wardrobe on the other. The walls were painted a dull green, giving a gloomy feel to the room. The bed was lumpy and uncomfortable and squeaked every time she rolled over. It reminded her of a Sunday school outing she had once been on, based in an outdoor pursuits centre, when she was five years old. She recalled a similar storm raging all those years ago, and the bed had creaked. She winced with the memory. She had screamed so much that her parents had to come in the middle of the night to take her home. Everyone was angry with her, telling her she needed to grow up and be less like a baby.

Céline set her jaw determinedly. She had come this far, she must face the future with courage and conviction. She peeled herself out of bed and put on some trousers and a thick woollen jumper. It felt like the weather had changed from summer to winter overnight. She pulled a brush through her tangled mass of hair and glanced in the mirror. She looked tired and grey. Looking at her watch, she was shocked to see that it was already eight-thirty. The darkness outside gave the impression that it was still the middle of the night. She climbed down the wooden stairs into the kitchen. Pascal and Sophia were just finishing their breakfast.

'I'm sorry I'm so late, I thought it was…'

'*Bonjour*, Céline, please don't worry, you must have been exhausted after your trip,' Pascal said kindly. 'I'm surprised that you managed to sleep through all this racket. We often get a strong wind here, called the *tramontane*. It starts in Biscay, I believe, and then it blows over the Pyrenees, picking up the freezing air of the snowy mountains.'

Céline was drawn to his unusual appearance. Pascal had a strikingly pale complexion, his white face framed by white-blond hair; even his eyelashes and eyebrows were white, almost invisible. He had the palest blue eyes she had ever seen, with a curious pink tinge to them, and his pupils flitted from side to side disconcertingly as he spoke. She wondered if he was blind.

'I see you're surprised by my appearance,' he said quietly. 'Don't worry, it's not a disease. I'm albino. It just means that my body doesn't produce enough melatonin. I have to take care in the sun, which is a shame because I spend most of my time outside tending the vines. But I wear a hat and overalls, and sunscreen, of course, and most of the time it isn't a problem at all.'

Céline stared at the floor, concerned that she had made him feel uncomfortable.

'I've got used to people either staring at me or looking the other away. I don't mind; in fact, I feel sorry for them, they probably feel more embarrassed than I do. My crazy eye movements seem to fascinate people. Luckily, my brain takes care of all that. Heaven alone knows how, but it does.' He paused. 'My vision is poor, sometimes blurry, but I see *you*,' he said, with a grin.

Not knowing quite how to respond, Céline turned to study Sophia. She had a heart-shaped face, dark eyes, an olive complexion, and lips that turned up at the edges, giving the impression that she was always smiling. Her shiny black shoulder-length hair fell in loose curls and bounced when she moved. But it was a large dark birthmark on the right side of her forehead that drew

Céline's attention: a mark that could easily be concealed with a fringe or makeup, but it somehow added to her striking appearance. Céline wondered if she had any Spanish blood in her. She was beautiful.

'My husband has taken a shine to you already!' Sophia said, her eyes twinkling.

Céline blushed, finding herself lost for words.

Sophia, sensing her embarrassment, swiftly changed the subject. 'Pascal and the workers have so much to do at this time of the year. They work from dawn until dusk, gathering up the last of the grapes and preparing the stripped vines for the winter months. We have a party to celebrate the gathering of the harvest in a week's time. It's usually a great celebration with a live band, delicious food and, of course, an abundance of fine local wines.' She rubbed her hands together in delight. 'The workers look forward to it every year. I hope you'll stay with us until after the party. Actually, I could do with some help organising the evening. I need to go to the local market and select some hams, cheeses and vegetables, organise the band and the marquee, and order a few crates of beer. And, I'm sure there will be a host of other things that I've totally forgotten about.' Her face shone with excited energy. 'Will you help me, Céline?'

'I would love to, Sophia,' Céline replied, crossing her arms in front of her chest and giving a sudden shiver. She moved closer to the open fire and stretched out the palms of both hands. The flames on a bed of smouldering wood provided welcome heat and cast a cheery glow across the kitchen.

'We are fortunate,' Sophia said, 'our bedroom is just over the chimney breast so we are always comfortably warm. I would imagine your room was rather draughty last night.'

'It wasn't too bad, but perhaps I could block some draughty cracks around the windows with some kitchen roll?'

'What a good idea,' Pascal said, reaching into a drawer and handing her a roll. 'We don't often have guests, and we certainly haven't got enough money to buy new windows. Why don't you relax today, keep warm and explore the house? We all call the place *la vieille maison* – the old house.' He shrugged his shoulders. 'Just because it's old. It used to be a château; it has thick stone walls but, like churches, the cold permeates the walls and it can feel very chilly. In summer, this is great because, even if the air is hot and humid outside, the house is always cool.'

'Please don't worry about me, I will enjoy finding my bearings. I have a good book to read and my computer here, I might even do some writing.'

Sophia shot her a glance. 'What do you write about?'

'I'm not sure yet. I'm still waiting for inspiration.' She looked into Sophia's steely eyes and remembered what Nicole had said. But her first impressions of Pascal and Sophia were that they were both welcoming and friendly. 'It's very kind of you both to invite me to stay, and I look forward to helping to organise the harvest party.'

'I have a dentist appointment this morning.' Sophia wrinkled up her nose. 'I simply loathe the dentist, but I must go. I shouldn't be gone long but, if you have time, it would be great if you would stack the dishwasher and generally tidy up the kitchen.'

'Sophia, perhaps we could let Céline relax today before…'

'No, I'm happy to do this,' Céline interrupted. 'It would make me feel more at home, it's the least I can do.'

'Okay, thanks. Do help yourself to tea and coffee, I think there are some of my favourite biscuits in the tin over there,' he said, pointing to a colourful biscuit barrel positioned next to the espresso machine. 'I shall be working in the fields all day today.' He glanced out of the window. 'The wind seems to have died down and the rain has stopped. The storms are usually worse at night.' He stood up, smiled and stepped out into the semi-darkness of the morning.

'Right, I must go too. Have a good day.'

Reluctantly, she moved away from the warmth and comfort of the fire to complete her domestic duties. The kitchen was the most welcoming room in the house, mainly because of the open fire and the colourful decorated pottery thoughtfully arranged on wooden shelves mounted on brackets, rather too high for her to reach but attractive, nonetheless. The sideboards were cluttered with condiments, herbs and spices, and open recipe books. A large wooden table stood in the centre of the uneven flagstone floor, strewn with paperwork; everything from bank statements to personal letters and magazines. The vintage Belfast sink caught Céline's eye. It was deep with elegant old-fashioned brass taps and cut into a dark pine cupboard and draining board. A large green Aga lookalike called La Cornue took pride of place, its heavy cast-iron frame creating warmth as well as cooking food. The room was a fine mix of old and new; modern gleaming white goods sitting comfortably beside old-fashioned cupboards and worktops.

Having tidied up, she left the cheeriness of the kitchen and explored the rest of the house. The dining room and sitting room were sparsely furnished with dark antique furniture, probably worth a lot of money a few years ago, but not as popular now. The wooden floors were covered with a variety of well-worn Indian rugs. Faded velvet curtains hung limply from tasselled pelmets. Worn chairs and a chaise longue were randomly arranged around an open fireplace that appeared not to have been used for years. The dining room had a rather splendid walnut table and chairs, and a free-standing standard lamp, but very little else. In her mind's eye, Céline could imagine a sumptuous and lively banquet taking place in this room back in historical times, but now, sadly, it was just a room that needed considerable refurbishment. The cloakroom was spacious with a lavatory with a chain and handle, reminding her of why we often talk about "pulling the chain", even though it is usually a modern lever nowadays. It was dark in every room, gloomy and lacklustre. There were five spacious bedrooms upstairs, again, all sparsely furnished and all but three rooms piled high with stuff: old suitcases, books and unused linen and towels. Céline breathed in the overpowering smell of mothballs, mustiness and disinfectant.

Pascal and Sophia's bedroom was considerably more homely with a large double bed, a window dresser and ensuite facilities. The room adjacent to their bedroom was a small dressing room, crammed full of Sophia's clothes: colourful dresses, tailored trousers and stylish jumpers, all strewn carelessly onto the bed. Céline had never seen so many pairs of shoes as Sophia had, all displayed on a shoe rack.

Finally, she went into the bathroom. The bath was free-standing, raised on ornamental animal claws. The basin was bowl shaped and mounted on a wooden surface which had discoloured due to water seepage over the years. In the corner stood an upright set of weighing scales, with weights that, when balanced, give an accurate body weight. Céline looked at these with a mixture of interest and dread. She had suffered from anorexia nervosa in her teens and she still felt the need to weigh herself every day, but this hadn't been possible for the last few weeks so she would wait until tomorrow morning when her stomach was empty before finding out how much she weighed.

Finally, she returned to her bedroom and noticed her rucksack in the corner where she had left it. She bit her lip, thinking how careless she had been. All her money, coins and gold bullion were stored there and in a money belt lying next to it. She searched the room for a suitable hiding place. As she stepped on the wooden floor by her bed, she faltered on a creaking floorboard beneath her feet. She stepped on it again; it was definitely loose. If she could prise it up, it might reveal a suitable hiding place. She rolled back the rug and sneezed from a cloud of dust that filled her nostrils. She reached into her back pocket and pulled out her Swiss Army Knife. Pushing the short blade in between the two boards, she carefully prised it upwards until finally the board came away. It felt as if the floorboard hadn't been disturbed for years. She sighed with satisfaction. Putting the penknife back in her pocket, she bent over and reached into the cavity. It would indeed be an ideal hiding place. Rolling up her sleeves, she explored further until she felt an object, round, smooth and cold to touch. She grasped it gently and pulled it out. She held the object in her cupped hands and her eyes widened in wonderment. It was a snow globe, covered in dust, which obscured the scene inside the glass. She rubbed the rounded surface with the edge of her linen sheet until the scene was revealed. As she shook the globe, snowflakes fell on a young couple: a man wearing a distinctive hat and both wearing long winter coats, walking hand in hand through a deep layer of snow. It was simple and yet truly exquisite. Céline shook it once again, marvelling at the beauty of this extraordinary find.

As an afterthought, she bent over once more and extended her arm further into the cavity until she discovered something else; it felt like a book. She carefully eased it out and blew the dust off the cover. It was a bound journal with gold-edged pages. She opened the front cover and a series of documents scattered across the floor around her.

Chapter 9

Mr Isaac Goldmann. His name was clearly inscribed on the inside of the front cover. She carefully turned to the first page. It appeared to be a handwritten journal, with diary entries spanning from 1937 to 1944. She realised, with disappointment, that the text, although immaculately scribed, was in German, and her knowledge and understanding of the language was poor. She surmised that it was written by Isaac Goldmann, a young man who had resided in the château during the latter months of the war. But why had he abruptly stopped recording diary entries? And what was he doing here? Was he working in the vineyard? Was he a refugee fleeing persecution? Isaac Goldmann. It sounded like a Jewish name.

She put the journal down and picked up the snow globe once again. As she shook the glass ball, her eyes focussed on the two people: a man and a woman, hand in hand. If only she could read German fluently, she would maybe discover the life story of this young man and his experiences before and during the war. She resolved to translate what appeared to be a fairly detailed account of seven years of his life. Her imagination ran wild; this could be a fascinating historical insight into the life of an individual; perhaps Jewish, perhaps a worker in the vineyard, perhaps a frightened young man fleeing persecution. Or death.

Placing the snow globe on her bedside table, she hugged the journal close to her chest. She would research the best translation tool to use on her computer, and she would scribe the text, word by word. It would take a long time, it would be challenging, but she could hardly wait to begin.

After mulling over her discovery, she decided it would be best not to mention this to Pascal or Sophia because firstly, they would realise that she was hiding something herself. And secondly, they would probably hand the journal over to the authorities, or to a historical museum, and the last thing she wanted to do was draw attention to herself in any way. No. It would remain her secret. For the time being.

Her body tensed as she heard the key turn in the lock of the front door. She hurriedly put the precious journal, the snow globe, most of her cash, gold coins, bullion and her money belt into the dark cavity, and replaced the floorboard quietly and with care, finally putting the rug back in place. She hugged herself in anticipation; she was intrigued and excited about the task ahead. Isaac Goldmann might have been a fugitive in hiding. Perhaps she would even discover some parallels with her own life.

'Céline,' Sophia called from the hallway. '*Voulez-vous du café?*'

'*Oui, merci*,' she replied brightly as she made her way to the kitchen. 'How was the dentist?'

'Not nearly as bad as I thought. I had no fillings this time,' she said, as she pressed the button on the espresso machine. 'I hope you like it strong?'

'The stronger the better,' replied Céline gratefully.

The two of them sat opposite each other and focussed for a few moments on sipping the hot reviving liquid. Sophia rummaged under the piles of paperwork and brought out a spiral-bound notebook and a Biro. 'You and I have some serious planning to do,' she said, her dark eyes twinkling with pleasure. 'But first, we need some lunch.' She went to the fridge and selected a variety of cheeses: Brie, creamy goats' cheese and Old Gouda. She arranged the cheese on a butcher's block and added some celery sticks, radishes and wedges of crispy lettuce. Finally, she broke some baguette into generous chunks and added a bowl of crisps. 'I hope this is enough for you, Céline. Usually Pascal comes in from the fields ravenous, but today he is not coming back until early this evening. He wants to get as much work done, before the storm clouds gather once again.'

She looked at the feast in front of her. 'This is perfect. Thanks, Sophia. Are you expecting another storm tonight?'

'Almost certainly, and the worst is yet to come, I'm afraid. Hopefully it will blow over before the harvest party in a few days' time.' She crossed her fingers and raised an eyebrow. 'If it doesn't, we'll just have to make do. We've had harvest celebrations in the marquee in ferocious storms before, and they have always been very atmospheric... if a little damp.'

Céline smiled. Sophia spoke to her as if she was French: the words flew out of her mouth at lightning speed, her smooth-as-honey voice rising and falling like a bird in flight. She made no attempt to speak slowly or use simple vocabulary, although she was quick to correct if Céline's French wasn't quite right.

After enjoying a sumptuous selection of bread and cheese, Sophia put an inviting plate of sliced watermelon in the middle of the table. 'We need to look after our health,' she said, putting her hands either side of her slim waist. 'I eat like a horse. I eat just as much as Pascal, and he's burning all those calories digging the land.'

The flames flickered in the fireplace, and even though it was only two o'clock in the afternoon, the light was fading outside and the wind was picking up. 'We'll need to batten down the hatches tonight, that's for sure. Now,' she said, retrieving her notebook. 'We need to make a list of food and drinks for the party. It's a funny thing about lists,' she said. 'It makes me feel I'm in control when I have written everything down that I need, but then I often forget to take the list.' She banged the side of her head gently with the palm of her hand. 'Sometimes I wonder why I bother, but here goes…' She reeled off a long list of food: cooked hams, cheeses, salami, chicken wings, guinea fowl, tinned duck, and pâté… She put her pen down and glanced upwards. 'Have you ever been to a French market?'

'Not for many years.'

'The market is a way of life for us. It's where we buy most of our food; the quality of the produce is outstanding, and the wide variety of different food is incredible. The locals are happy to queue for hours at their favourite butcher or cheese counter because they know that the delicacies that they select will be well worth the wait. And the shopkeepers know and value their customers.'

'It sounds great. I usually go to the supermarket for my weekly shop.'

Sophia wrinkled her nose. 'I go to the supermarket as rarely as possible. I pick up the basics, but the quality and variety cannot be compared. And they use too much plastic.'

'You are right, Sophia, a lot of people don't like plastic wrappers. I look forward to going to the market.'

'Good, we'll go tomorrow morning. I think we should make an early start to beat the queues. Now, I haven't thought about any drinks for the party yet. Of course, we will have a rich selection of our own vintage, mainly red, but we do have some white and rosé as well. We probably should pick up a few crates of beer. Some of the workers actually prefer beer to wine,' she said, laughing. 'We sell our produce at some of the local markets and always make a good profit. The French are very keen to support local businesses.'

She jotted down a few more items on her list, and then she placed it in the middle of a chaotic pile of paperwork. She smiled wryly. No wonder Sophia often forgot to take her list. Céline retired to her bedroom for the rest of the afternoon. She researched the most accurate translation tool, downloaded the application, and soon she was ready to begin her project.

As she documented the first diary entry, the story of Isaac Goldmann started to emerge:

3 September 1937

We live in troubled times. There is civil unrest sweeping across Germany. In my hometown, Konstanz, people live in fear. German police officials have rounded up convicted offenders and incarcerated them in concentration camps not far from here. We in the Jewish community are not safe. Thousands of Jews have been murdered in a concentration camp near Weimar. I must flee from my hometown, the place where I was born and raised. It is with deep sadness that I must leave my dearest parents behind. They are steadfast in their belief that they must stay, uphold their beliefs, and support and protect their homeland. It breaks my heart, but I must respect their wishes. I might never see them again. I have all the papers I need, and I intend to head for Marseille by train tomorrow. With God's speed, I will escape the shores of France and make the hazardous voyage across the Atlantic to America.

As Céline digested the words on the page, her eyes filled with tears. His words were poignant and desperately sad. She resolved to research this period of history in Germany and France to provide a context – a backdrop – for what Isaac Goldmann had to say.

After supper, Céline decided to get an early night. She lay in bed and listened to the raging gale and driving rain lashing on the window panes. Thankfully, the strategically positioned kitchen roll – rather like the caulking on a wooden ship – had dulled the rattling sound between the glass and the window frame, but there was still a cold draught that chilled the bedroom. She pulled the covers over her bare shoulders and shivered; she was surprised that Pascal and Sophia still used sheets and blankets, rather than duvets, but she was thankful for the warmth and weight of the linen sheets and woollen blankets that tucked snugly around her body. She fought against the well-stuffed bolster pillow to find a comfortable position for her head and neck – it felt like a brick – but eventually she fell into a fitful sleep.

All of a sudden, the light on the landing went out and the room was plunged into complete darkness. She looked up but she could see nothing except the black of the night. She heard a gentle knock on her door, and someone peered into the room and whispered, 'I'm afraid the wind has taken down the power lines, so I've brought you a box of candles and some matches. There are extra blankets in the cupboard if you need them. This often happens at this time of the year unfortunately.'

Céline blinked her eyes and peered at Sophia, her face eerily lit up by the small flickering flame of a candle. 'It shouldn't take long to get it fixed but, for tonight, we'll just have to make do. I must stoke the fire early tomorrow morning so we don't all freeze.' With that, she padded back onto the landing, closing the door behind her.

The storm continued all night, and Céline wondered if there had been any structural damage to the house, or whether any trees had blown down. She hoped not. Lying still and holding in the warmth of her body beneath the blankets, she glanced towards the window: a tiny chink of light crept in from beneath the curtains, heralding the dawn of a new day.

Chapter 10

'It's breakfast time,' Sophia called from the hallway.

As Céline opened the door to the kitchen, she was welcomed by Sophia. Today she wore a bright-red polka-dot dress with a tight-fitting bodice, drawn in at the waist and flaring out to just above the knee. It was stylish but rather old-fashioned and reminded Céline of what her mother used to wear.

'The power's still down, I'm sorry to say, so it's muesli for us today. I can't even make a coffee, but we'll be able to pick up an espresso at the market. I'm not even going to ask you if you had a good night,' she said quietly. 'Never mind, the market will cheer us up. Pascal is taking wine to a local wine merchant this morning so he's got the van. I'll be driving the old Renault 4. It's a great car, but it isn't always reliable...' Sophia stared forlornly at the coffee machine. 'If only I could arm myself with a good strong coffee for the journey... but we'll be fine.'

Céline was feeling less than reassured by Sophia, but she looked forward to a morning at the local market nonetheless. Just as they were leaving the house, she reminded Sophia about her list.

'I knew I'd forget!' Sophia said cheerily, turning

back into the kitchen to search for the single piece of paper.

The car was light blue, with narrow wheels and a practical and spacious interior. Céline wondered whether it was a classic car. It was obviously much loved, but an old banger. Every time the car drove over a pothole or a bump in the road, her back jarred with pain. The wind had eased and the rain had stopped as they pulled into the uneven track leading to the market. Eventually, the car came to a standstill with an abrupt jerk.

The low grey clouds scudded across the sky as the two women grasped a wicker basket in each hand and strode towards the square. Céline was surprised at how many stalls were already set up, and how many locals were busily weaving in and out of the narrow aisles, studying the inviting array of food. She was drawn to a display of tomatoes. Not just one variety, but a hugely impressive selection: massive beef tomatoes, greeny-red tomatoes, cherry tomatoes, uneven tomatoes, tomatoes on the vine… She turned to the next stall: the local butcher. This was undoubtedly the most popular stall. There was already a queue forming, mainly elderly women, carrying their baskets, chatting, and patiently waiting for their turn. They knew that the meat was worth the long wait. Céline watched from afar as the butcher prepared *foie de veau* – calf liver – with meticulous care, removing every tiny morsel of fat, before weighing it and showing it proudly to the customer. He then wrapped it carefully in paper advertising his business. Most of the locals bought a rich variety of meat: everything from cheap cuts of beef – *plat de côte pour faire un Pot au Feu* – to stuffed quail. Most of the elderly customers paid in cash, and the butcher carefully packed their purchases in the baskets and had a little chat to pass the time of day before turning to the next customer. Céline smiled; it wouldn't be good to visit the market if you were in a hurry.

She was aware that Sophia was on a mission to buy the food needed for the harvest party, and it gave her some time to explore the market stalls. She was surprised to pass the horse butcher, exclusively selling a variety of cuts of lean horse meat. But more tempting was the mouth-watering aroma of the rotisserie chicken and pork belly wafting in the air. Most of the chickens had been pre-ordered and they were disappearing fast. She feasted her eyes on the roast potatoes sizzling in trays underneath the plump rotisserie chickens. She decided to treat Pascal and Sophia to a few slices of succulent pork and crackling. She handed a few euros over to the ruddy-faced shopkeeper, thinking that a few chunks of pork might help to keep them warm during another cold night.

She watched as the locals carefully inspected the fruit and vegetables before they handed over their money. They held punnets of French strawberries to their noses to smell the sweet scent and to check that they were buying the tastiest varieties. They chose the plumpest figs and the rosiest of apples. Céline could see how food was a very important aspect of their daily life – almost a religion – and how discerning the customers were.

The fresh, rounded face of the woman behind the cheese counter looked just like the rounds of creamy goats' cheese and freshly churned butter that she was selling. She looked wholesome and healthy, just like her cheese. The proprietor, meanwhile, was eating a chunk of Old Gouda and enjoying a glass of red wine with his friends. The selection of cheese was out of this world, selling Comté of all different ages, from twelve to thirty-six months; goats' cheese and sheep cheese. She wondered how on earth they packed away the leftover produce ready for the next market. They must be determined to make their business a success by selling their tempting wares, and, by the look of the queue, it was working.

But it was the fish counter that most drew Céline's attention. There were many varieties of fish and crustaceans displayed, all freshly caught, with gleaming eyes. She noticed that none of the bass were as big as the one that Jacques had caught, but they were still beautiful specimens. She was fascinated by a bowl of tiny white shrimps called *crevette blanche*. She couldn't resist buying a small bag to taste. Each little shrimp gave a burst of flavour so intense that it reminded her of her childhood.

Just at the entrance to the market was a small stall selling honey from the local beekeeper. She sighed with pleasure. If only she had more time and more cash to indulge in some of the local delicacies displayed.

In amongst the crowd she caught sight of Sophia, her baskets brimming over with goodies. She was having a lively conversation with a small group of friends. She beckoned Céline over to them.

'There's a small café over the road. I'm gasping for an espresso.' She said goodbye to her friends and took Céline firmly by the arm. At last they could rest their weary legs and enjoy an espresso, a glass of water and a *pain au raisin*.

'Did you find everything on the list, Sophia?'

'Yes, I think so. I will go to the supermarket this afternoon and buy the crates of beer and anything else that I've forgotten. I can manage, you don't need to come with me. Oh, and can you remind me to order ten baguettes from the bakery? They will deliver them on the day.'

Céline looked around the simple café. It was mostly full of elderly gentlemen drinking beer or coffee and meeting friends. She wondered wryly if their wives were still queuing at the butcher or the cheese counter.

Refreshed and nourished, they headed back to the car, Sophia bending under the weight of her shopping. It had been a very successful trip to the market.

Céline, determined to make the most of the time she had to herself after lunch, gazed out of her bedroom window at the grounds. The storm clouds had now dispersed, overtaken by a deep-blue sky and a few fluffy clouds. It was as if the sky had been cleaned by the recent storms. She had already explored the inside of the house, but the inclement weather had prevented her from venturing outside. Now was her chance.

She closed the main door to the old house and stepped out into the grounds, which were largely bare except for one or two hardy shrubs that had survived the fierce heat of the summer. The rain of the last two days had almost disappeared, leaving a thin, muddy film on the otherwise parched earth. She closed her eyes and absorbed the heat of the sun, pleasantly warm on her cheeks. The last couple of days had felt bleak and cold, but this afternoon it felt like a warm summer's day.

Turning back to study the house, she thought it looked rather ramshackle, but it had a certain beauty and charm; a French rustic manor house, with yellow-and-beige weathered stone walls and brown shutters, many of which were closed to maintain the temperature inside. A single woody plant clung to the front wall, forming an impressive, tangled web of branches and autumnal orange and gold leaves, spreading outwards and upwards, and breathing its life into the guttering. The roof itself was covered in thick terracotta tiles, with a line of striking cockscomb on the uppermost ridge. A single chimney stack rose from the left of the house. But it was the large and impressive wooden front door – arched and intricately carved – that provided the centrepiece of the formidable house.

As she followed the path leading to the backyard, she was greeted by a few inquisitive chickens and a large fierce-looking cockerel, scrabbling around her feet, hopeful of a few grains of corn. Walking some distance away from the back of the house, she discovered, to her surprise, a gated area with a kidney-shaped swimming pool, surrounded by white paving slabs, a modern outdoor shower and a couple of sunbeds. Céline opened the gate set in a wall and lifted one edge of the blue plastic pool cover. She peered underneath. The water looked clean and inviting and any dead leaves had been removed. She passed her fingers through the warm silky water, wondering who maintained this area so fastidiously. She stood up, shook her hand dry, and gazed at the surrounding area. To one side there was a line of young olive trees, and to the other a row of cypress trees standing proud and tall, reminding Céline of sentries standing to attention; they gave privacy to anyone enjoying the facilities. She would ask Pascal if she could have an early dip one morning; she loved swimming, and the pool looked very inviting.

As she left the gated area, something gleaming in the sun caught her eye. She crouched down and examined the simple and ingenious way in which the pool was heated by the sun. A black hosepipe had been threaded through a snaking line of bottomless and clear wine bottles, that magnified the sun on the black hosepipe. Water from the swimming pool was pumped through the pipe, heated by the sun, and then ran back into the pool. She smiled. What a great way of capturing the warm rays of the sun and making very good use of empty white wine bottles.

Returning to the front of the house, she manoeuvred her way past the flock of chickens and walked towards the rickety gate that defined the boundary of the property. Her eyes widened as she gazed at the sheer beauty of the vineyard: the individual black twisted vines ablaze with colour – yellow gold and deep red – set out neatly in straight symmetrical lines, stretching as far as the eye could see.

She wandered over to a low stone building, like an outhouse or barn. The entrance appeared to be well used; there were no cobwebs or overgrown weeds. She lifted the old wooden latch and peered inside. As her eyes acclimatised to the darkness, she noticed in the far corner a low-level camp bed, a candle and matches, and a collection of glasses. She wondered whether this was used by the workers as a place to socialise. The base of the outhouse was bare soil, and a few barrels were stored at the far end on a wooden pallet. Céline raised her eyebrows. The outhouse looked rather like the gamekeeper's cottage in *Lady Chatterley's Lover*. She tutted to herself; her imagination was running wild.

She looked at her watch and gasped, the time had flown and it would soon be supper time. She had planned to do more translation but that would have to wait for another day. She paused to gaze once again at the vineyard, as the burnt orange of the sun slowly disappeared behind the distant foothills of the Pyrenees.

Chapter 11

Saturday morning dawned bright and clear. Today was the day. The old house was a lively hubbub of activity, and by mid-afternoon preparations were well under way for the harvest party. Pascal and Sophia, helped by some of the workers, had positioned a number of long trestle tables and benches in the large dusty outside area. A huge rusty fire pit, well stacked with kindling and firewood – vine roots – provided a focal point, surrounded by half-barrels and logs for seating, leaving a large open area for dancing. The facade of the old house was adorned with fairy lights and colourful bunting. The pathway leading to the gate at the entrance was lined by solar lights, positioned to welcome the guests to join the celebrations.

'Hi, Céline. How does it look? We're so lucky with the weather,' Sophia said, looking up at the cloudless sky. 'There's no need for the marquee today, thank goodness. We'll put the buffet, wine and beer on tables in the kitchen, and people can help themselves. We'll be dancing under the stars tonight,' she said, her chest heaving with pleasure.

'It looks great! How many people are you expecting?'

'About twenty, I would imagine, if all the workers bring their wives, husbands... or lovers, of course,' she added with a wink. 'Now, I must get on. I've got to think about what the musicians might need. We've got Marc and Simone playing tonight. They are a dynamic duo: Marc plays the guitar and squeeze box, and Simone is a fiddle player. They sing harmonies together. Between them, they do a good line in banter, and usually bring the house down! We'll be singing and dancing the night away.'

Sophia's excitement was infectious and everyone rallied round, chattering nineteen to the dozen. Céline was left feeling like a spare part. She realised she could either run around trying to look busy or retire to her bedroom and do some more translation. She discreetly made her way to the sanctuary of her room, opened her computer and retrieved the precious journal from under the floorboards. She eagerly turned to the next entry in Isaac Goldmann's diary:

23 March 1941

I realise I have been neglectful of my journal. I have been busy enjoying life in Marseille, but sadly, I must always remain vigilant. There are many French officials here, keen to hand over any so-called "degenerates" to the Nazis, always trying to court favour with them. I am staying at the home of an elderly Jewish couple – Jacob and Eva – dear friends of my parents. They are kind and generous, sheltering Jewish people who are trying to escape to Palestine or America. The house is on three floors, in one of the many side streets leading to the Old Port. My room is small and basic, and I share all the facilities, but it is adequate for my needs. Something quite remarkable has happened to me. My heart has been touched by a beautiful American woman called Beth. Now I understand the true meaning of love. I can't stop thinking about her. Quite by chance, she works for an organisation that helps people to leave France and escape to the safety of America. At last, I can breathe again. At last, I feel optimistic about my future.

Céline lay on her bed and closed her eyes, blissfully dreaming about a passionate love affair between two people: Beth and Isaac Goldmann. She dozed for about an hour or so before waking up with a start. She hurriedly replaced the journal and her computer and went downstairs and into the kitchen. There she found a sumptuous feast laid out on two large tables. Open bottles of wine: red, white and rosé, a bucket of ice, and dozens of glasses had been placed on another table positioned against the wall.

Outside, the light had faded and the solar lights cast a warm rosy glow, lighting up the pathway to the entrance of the old house. The fairy lights twinkled cheerfully from the midst of the climbing plant that grew against the front wall. She turned to face the fire pit, now alight; the vine roots crackled, the white-orange flames blazed, and a plume of smoke curled up towards the early evening sky. Everything was ready.

Céline hurried back upstairs, threw off her clothes, and got into the shower. The hot water took time to clunk through the antiquated system, but eventually she was able to enjoy the warm water as it trickled over the nape of her neck. The party was about to begin and she had mixed feelings about it. She felt like an interloper. She had not been involved in the growing of the grapes or in the gathering of the harvest. Did she deserve to celebrate alongside those who had? Her French, although quite fluent, was not good enough to understand fast colloquial speech. She was an outsider. Lathering the lavender soap suds deep into her skin, she decided she would put her worries aside and enjoy the party. It would be a good opportunity to get to know some of the workers, and perhaps learn something about the art of winemaking.

She selected a burnished-gold knee-length dress that clung to her body in all the right places. She had bought the dress in Marseille when she went shopping with Nicole. She delved deeper into her wardrobe and chose a chocolate-brown cashmere wrap to drape around her bare shoulders. Although the day had been warm, the temperatures usually dropped significantly at dusk. She drew her hair into a messy bun, secured with a gold scrunchie, and sprayed her neck liberally with *Calèche*. To complete her look, she pulled on a pair of black pumps and looked in the mirror. She could hardly recognise her own reflection. Removing a single strand of hair from her sun-kissed face, she was surprisingly satisfied with her appearance. Now she was ready.

People were starting to gather, glass in hand, around the blazing fire. Sophia, standing in the midst of a group, held court and Céline could see the overt adoration on the faces of the men and women surrounding her. This evening she wore a white blouse with puff sleeves and a colourful flouncy skirt. Céline observed her captivating her audience, her voice rising and falling.

It was as if she was reciting a sonnet or singing a love song. She stopped abruptly when she saw Céline, her dark eyes dancing with pleasure. '*Ma belle, allez-y,*' Sophia beckoned, skilfully drawing Céline into the conversation with friendly introductions and cheerful banter. Céline felt her shoulders relax as she sipped her wine, allowing the conversation to drift over her head and into the air. She quietly absorbed the unique atmosphere of a vineyard party, set deep in the Southern French countryside. This promised to be a memorable evening.

She turned to see Pascal sitting alone on a wooden bench, occasionally lifting a small bottle of beer to his lips. 'It's a great gathering, isn't it?' she called.

He looked up, and then patted the bench beside him. 'Would you like to come and keep me company for a while?'

'Of course, Pascal, it would be my pleasure,' she answered, surprised that he was all alone. 'Aren't we lucky that the storms of the last few days have passed? It is such a beautiful calm evening, and it's still quite warm,' she added, slipping the wrap from her shoulders.

'The *tramontane* winds never last for more than a few days, but yes, I am pleased. This evening is ideal weather for hosting a party.' He paused. 'I've just been thinking about how hard we have all worked in the fields this year, but the fruit on the vine is our reward; we have a bountiful harvest,' he said, 'and the grapes will be made into exceptional wine.'

Céline took a sip of the succulent red liquid and

licked her lips. 'If it's anywhere near as tasty as this wine, it will be truly excellent.' She looked sideways. Pascal was watching Sophia as she shone and delighted her audience. 'Poor Sophia has hardly seen me. Some days, I leave before dawn and return late into the evening. It is still busy in the autumn and winter months, but less so than in the spring or summer. I will make it up to her.'

She heard the sadness in his voice as he spoke, his flickering eyes still focussing on his wife. 'I'm sure you will, Pascal, and, as you say, the hard work has paid off. Wouldn't it be so much worse if, after all the hard graft and long hours, the crop was poor and you had nothing to show for it?' She smiled benevolently. 'I haven't known you for very long, but Sophia seems happy and content. And she is strikingly beautiful, isn't she?'

'I have always felt that she is too good for me,' he said sadly, 'but when I'm with her, I spoil her and try to make her feel special. And love her with all my heart.'

The conversation was becoming rather uncomfortable, so Céline decided to change the subject. 'Do all these people work in the vineyard, or are some of them friends and neighbours?'

'Most of them are employed here, either working full- or part-time. And others are neighbours who are part of the wine cooperative and are fellow wine growers. We have friendly competition, but we still share ideas on how to improve our crops and keep disease at bay.'

'Wow, it's obviously quite a technical process making wine. I thought it was just a case of fermenting the grape juice and popping it into bottles.'

'You have a lot to learn, Céline,' he said with a smile.

'And I'm looking forward to finding out more about the whole process… I'm starting to feel rather peckish so I think I'll go and get some of that delicious buffet. How about you, Pascal?'

He smiled. 'I think I'll sit here a while longer, I do enjoy people-watching.'

Céline turned and wandered away towards the kitchen, selected a modest plate of cooked ham, and salad, refilled her wine glass, and sat on the bench in front of one of the empty trestle tables. Looking around, the party was now in full swing, with lots of animated conversation and laughter.

Suddenly, she froze. A deep shiver ran down her spine. She could feel a presence. Someone was watching her. She shook her head, her eyes fixed on her plate of food. It was probably nothing. Lifting her fork, she furtively glanced from one side to the other. She twisted her head sharply to look behind. It was then that she saw him. He locked eyes with her.

And then he was gone.

Chapter 12

She looked again, but there was no one there. Had he been a figment of her imagination? Were her eyes playing tricks on her? She had been anxious and stressed for some time, perhaps she had seen something that simply wasn't there. She gazed at the meal in front of her and realised that she had completely lost her appetite. Taking the plate of untouched food back into the kitchen, she clutched her wine to her chest and headed for the throng that had now gathered around the fire pit to enjoy the musical talents of Marc and Simone.

Simone stood up, swept her long auburn hair dramatically from her face, and placed her fiddle proudly under her chin. Swinging her bow high into the air, she paused, and then drew it across the lowest string, mellow and urgent. She meandered indulgently through the middle register, toying with every note, tantalising the audience, before reaching the final crescendo with an extravagant trill on the very highest note, the sweet sound cradled in the air before fading into the night. She stood erect, statuesque. The audience held their breath. Marc struck two rhythmic chords, and then the music began. Her Romani-style fiddle cut through the air in the midst of a thick cloud of rosin.

One by one, the people started to dance. Men and women alternately linked arms, elbow to elbow, and were passed from partner to partner. When the duo struck up a popular French anthem, everyone sang with gusto as they danced. Céline was reminded of a barn dance move, "strip the willow". She clapped her hands, stamped her feet, and admired the dancing from the sidelines. All of a sudden, she was dragged to one end of the line and was flung from one partner to the next, finally ending up with a flourish in the arms of a rather buxom lady.

Céline gently eased herself away from the jovial dancer and threw herself down on a log to catch her breath. It was then that she noticed something puzzling. Sophia was leaving the party and following the illuminated path to the gate. She quickly made her way across the yard so that she could see where Sophia was going, bumping into Pascal on the way. 'Is Sophia okay? She's heading for the vineyard, do you think she's getting more wine? Perhaps I should lend her a hand.'

'She's had a busy day, she probably needs a break. She often wanders off on her own.' He brushed past her, shrugging his shoulders. 'What she does is her own business.'

Céline, now intrigued, decided to follow Sophia from a distance. Making her way stealthily along the path and through the gate, she turned and, to her surprise, caught a glimpse of Sophia and a man with long dark hair disappearing into the outhouse, Sophia giggling as she closed the wooden door. Céline stared open-mouthed as she watched the shadows of two people in a passionate embrace, their bodies intertwined, barely illuminated by the flame of a solitary flickering candle.

Her body stiffened, captivated by the scene unfolding in front of her. But after a few minutes, she decided she should return to the party or she could be in danger of being discovered. Her head was buzzing with unanswered questions: who is the swarthy man that appeared to be Sophia's lover? Is he one of the workers, or perhaps a neighbour? As she made her way back towards the old house, she felt desperately sorry for Pascal. It appeared that his wife, who he obviously adored, was having an affair. Perhaps he already knew. He didn't seem at all concerned about where she was going.

Feeling hungry now, she returned to the kitchen. An elderly bespectacled gentleman greeted her with a smile. *'Bonsoir, je m'appelle Gaston.'*

'I'm Céline,' she replied cheerfully, 'I'm very pleased to meet you.'

'I zink you are English, no?'

'My mother was French and my father was English. I was brought up in England, but now I'm spending some time in France to get a flavour of where my mother lived when she was a child. Actually, she was born and brought up in the outskirts of Marseillan.'

'Well, well… It is a beautiful part of southwestern France, and considerably cheaper than the Riviera. I have lived here all my life. I wonder if I knew your mother. What was her name?'

'Émilie Dupont,' she replied, immediately concerned that she had given too much information away about her family to this friendly gentleman, but she needn't have worried. 'I have a memory like a sieve these days, but I don't remember anyone of that name. Are you enjoying your stay with Pascal and Sophia?'

'I'm having a great time, they are a nice couple.'

He nodded. 'Pascal is one in a million.'

Céline noted that he didn't mention Sophia. 'I feel very fortunate that my stay coincides with this incredible celebration of the grape harvest.'

'We always have a wonderful party, but it is not typical of many of the harvest events across France. Normally, the celebration of the grape harvest is a huge affair, involving whole towns or villages, with national dancing, competitions, wine tasting, barbecues, fairground rides for the children, and much more...' He paused to help himself to a chunk of Comté and some walnuts. 'We live in a small and remote commune here, deep in the French countryside. Marseillan is the nearest town, and it is twenty kilometres away. We enjoy a much smaller, more intimate affair, and the old house is a wonderful location. We always look forward to the party every year.'

'Do you work on the vines?'

'I'm too old now to work in the fields,' he said sagely. 'I offer advice, based on fifty years' experience, but do the younger generation listen? No, they don't. They have newfangled ideas about everything, and they always think they know best. I'm more traditional, I think the old methods were the best; they might not have been as productive, but they were simple, and there was less to go wrong. And there wasn't a computer in sight!'

'Do you have family here?'

His wrinkled face crumpled with pain. 'I have a son, Pierre. When he was young, he was full of beans, and bright...' He hesitated. 'He works here at the vineyard, but I'm sorry to say he has been badly influenced by... You don't want to hear my woes, especially not this evening.'

Céline looked at the sorry figure standing beside her. 'Carry on, Gaston. I really don't mind listening.' She wondered why people so often confided in her about their worries. 'What has happened to Pierre?'

'He has suffered depression for some years, but he has become belligerent and sullen in the last few months. I worry that he might be involved with drugs. I don't know for sure, but he has changed so much and it all started when he became friends with Luca.'

'Luca?'

'He is one of the workers here,' he said through clenched teeth. 'He is bad through and through... But what can I do? Pierre is twenty-four, he is old enough to know his own mind.' He stared at her, his eyes dull, his shoulders hunched. 'Let me give you some advice. If you come across Luca, have *nothing* to do with him.' He covered his face with his hands. 'He is rotten to the core.'

Céline thought carefully about how to respond, not wishing to upset this elderly gentleman more than he already was. 'I'm very sorry to hear this, and I will certainly take heed of what you tell me about Luca. I just hope that, for Pierre, this is just a passing phase. Maybe he could find a job in another vineyard?'

'He knows he can work in the vineyard nearby that I used to own, but he refuses point-blank. How I long to get my happy-go-lucky son back? His mother died many years ago when Pierre was nine years old, and, since then, we have always been like two strong brothers against the world. But now…'

'Tell me, Gaston, what does Luca look like?'

'He has a Spanish look about him, with long dark hair. A rough diamond. His looks are very distinctive, you really can't mistake him for anyone else. Some say he attracts women like bees to a honeypot.' He added on a lighter note, 'He's probably had more women than I've had hot dinners!'

Long dark hair. Céline furrowed her brow, trying to push dark thoughts to the back of her mind. She cupped both his hands in hers. 'Will you do me the honour of dancing with me?'

'Come on, no need to stand on ceremony,' he said, his deeply lined face breaking into a smile. '*Ooh la la*, would I turn down the chance of dancing with the most beautiful woman here?'

As they made their way to the dance area, Céline whispered in his ear, 'I'm staying with Pascal and Sophia for the next few days, so if you want to talk, I'm happy to listen.' As they danced, Céline could see him transform from a stooped, elderly man, to a lithe dancer, his face radiating pleasure.

Towards the end of the evening, Céline yawned. She was beginning to feel tired. The fast fiddle playing had become softer and more mellow, and she decided to rest her weary limbs by the fire pit, which had also died down, but the embers were glowing and it was comfortably warm. She perched on a half-barrel and listened to the low humming of the cicadas. It had been an interesting party, but she was still reeling from her discovery. What was Sophia up to? Was she having an affair with the infamous Luca?

All of a sudden, a stranger appeared out of the darkness. He took her firmly by the hand and pulled her to the dance area. A rough, calloused hand grasped her bare shoulder, the other encircled her waist, as he pulled her roughly towards him. He held her with a vice-like grip, so close that she could feel his masculine power. Her chest heaved with mounting desire, as she inhaled his musky scent and felt his muscular torso against her breast. Closing her eyes, she felt electric shocks of excitement and pleasure – like the tumultuous waves of a stormy sea – course through her body.

She dreamily blinked her eyes open and, to her horror, saw Sophia, rooted to the spot, hands on hips, glaring at them, her face etched with fury. Céline wrenched herself away from the arms of the stranger. She looked from him to her. And then she knew.

Chapter 13

After a sleepless night, Céline pulled herself out of bed and drew back the curtains. Outside, the debris from the night before had been left untouched; plates of half-eaten food and dirty glasses littered the tables, empty bottles of wine were strewn all over the ground, the fire pit was now grey and dirty. No one was about. She sighed. The chaotic scene in front of her looked like the *Mary Celeste*.

Céline felt gloom descend as she recalled the events of the night before, witnessing Sophia in a passionate embrace with her lover in the outhouse. She flinched as she remembered her conversation with Gaston: *If you come across Luca, have nothing to do with him...* She drew her hands roughly through her tangled hair as she recalled her dance with a stranger, the excitement and exhilaration, but then seeing Sophia's furious face. If he had not had his hair tied back, she would have recognised him.

Burying her head in her hands, Céline regretted the events of the night before. Had she had too much wine? She wasn't sure, but how she wished she could turn back the clock. She gazed into the distance as the orange-and-yellow sun rose majestically from the distant flatlands of the Languedoc to light up the dawn sky. She threw open the window, breathed in the fresh autumnal air, and felt fortified for the day ahead. She worried that Sophia might still be angry with her, but, for now, she would push it to the back of her mind and go for an early morning swim to clear her head. She slipped on her dressing gown and tiptoed down the stairs and out through the front door. The grounds were deserted as she made her way past the noisy flock of chickens to the back yard. She opened the gate to the swimming pool area, and, as she removed the cover she smiled, the pool looked inviting. She slipped out of her robe and edged herself into the clear water. It was just the right temperature: cool enough to energise her, but warm enough for her to swim a few lengths without shivering. She sighed with pleasure as the silky water caressed her naked body. All she could hear was the gentle rustling of leaves in the nearby cypress trees and the soft coo of a collared dove. The gloom of earlier had now lifted and she felt calm. After all, Sophia didn't know that she had witnessed the scene in the outhouse. As far as Sophia was concerned, Céline was just having a dance with one of the workers, she had no reason to be cross with her.

Sensing that someone was watching, she looked towards the old house. There, she saw Pascal looking out of his bedroom window, waving and smiling. A few minutes later, he appeared and, without hesitating, he plunged into the water. 'It is such a lovely time of the day for a dip, isn't it? Perfect for me, because the early morning sun doesn't harm my skin. Unfortunately, I don't often have time to swim before work. I hope you don't mind me joining you?'

'Of course not.' She laughed. 'It is your pool, after all.' She gazed beyond him. 'I thought I just saw someone over there by the cypress trees.'

'Ah, that might have been Luca coming to pick up the milk. The farmer leaves a couple of milk churns by the back gate. He's an early bird, Luca. He doesn't seem to need much sleep.'

Although curious to find out more about Luca, she gauged that now was not the time. 'There's a lot of clearing up to do after the party. I'm happy to make a start on this after breakfast.'

'Ah, you've reminded me, I need to ask you something.'

Céline held her breath. Had she done something wrong?

'I've noticed that Sophia is getting very tired recently, and I think she could do with some help around the house. Would you like to stay here for a while and do some light domestic duties? You could live rent-free and, on top of that, I'd pay you a small salary in cash? No pressure though.'

Céline breathed a sigh of relief. 'Thank you, it's a tempting proposal. Are you sure it's okay with Sophia?'

'Yes, of course. We've spoken about it and she would be grateful for your help. It would make me very happy too. I enjoy your company, Céline.'

'Well, in that case, my answer is yes,' she said. She enjoyed staying with Pascal and Sophia, although what had happened last night had cast a shadow.

'Great! That's settled then.' He scooped up some water and splashed Céline in the face. She gulped in surprise and promptly retaliated. They hooted with laughter, like excited children. She glanced back towards the old house, to see the silhouette of Sophia watching them intently from the window.

'Well, I think that's enough for me.' She watched as Pascal hoisted himself out of the pool, she had never seen skin as white. 'See you later, I'll tell Sophia the good news.' He threw a towel loosely over his shoulders and made his way back to the house.

Feeling refreshed, Céline climbed up the steps and, realising that she had forgotten her towel, drew her dressing gown over her wet body. After a quick shower, she got dressed, pulled a comb through her hair and went downstairs to have breakfast. Sophia greeted her with a frosty stare.

'*Bonjour*. Pascal tells me that you have agreed to stay here for a few weeks.'

'Yes,' Céline answered weakly. 'Although we didn't discuss how long I would stay. I'm happy to do anything I can to help.'

Sophia stared out of the window. 'Well, you can begin by clearing up the mess from last night. Outside looks like a scene of devastation. I'm going out this morning,' she said, as she turned and swept out of the room.

'Of course. I'll make a start after breakfast,' Céline called after her. She sank heavily into her chair and clutched her hot coffee cup in both hands. She wondered if she had made a terrible mistake, agreeing to stay. Sophia was obviously angry with her. Perhaps, if she did a thorough job of cleaning the house and grounds, Sophia would realise that the decision to ask her to stay had been a good one.

She worked non-stop for four hours, cleaning the entire house and the grounds. There was a lot of clearing up to be done; it was a mammoth task to do single-handed. When she had, at last, stacked the last trestle table away in the shed, she inspected her work, in the house and in the grounds. She was satisfied that she had done a good job; everything was back in place and everywhere looked pristine.

Sophia had not returned, so Céline made herself a well-earned cup of tea and went to her bedroom. Her whole body ached with exhaustion, and her back hurt. She would use her free time productively by finding out more about the life of Isaac Goldmann. She retrieved the journal from under the floorboards, opened the lid of her computer and started to read:

15 January 1943

My heart is broken. I must leave Marseille tonight under the cover of darkness. My hopes of sailing to America have been dashed. Yesterday, Beth's uncle had a tipoff which, if it came to pass, would have devastating consequences for our Jewish community. Under the Vichy regime, the German army, assisted by French police, have plans to raid the Old Port and round up and arrest all Jews. If I stay, I would almost certainly be transported to an extermination camp and killed. I have no choice, I must leave the town I have come to love. And I must bid farewell to the woman I love and adore.

Céline reflected on Isaac Goldmann's words. She found it hard to imagine the agony and pain he must have endured, to leave behind everything he loved and to flee for his life. She read the words over and over again, tears flowing freely down her cheeks. She felt privileged to read a personal account of someone who lived during a historical period of human atrocity. She closed the journal with great care and hugged it close to her chest. If only we could change the course of history. If only everything had been different for Isaac and Beth.

'Céline, are you here?' called Sophia from the hallway.

'Hi, Sophia. I'll be down in a minute.' She hurriedly replaced the journal in its hiding place and closed down her computer.

She found Sophia in the kitchen making a cup of coffee. She turned with a bright smile. 'You've done a great job of clearing up after the party, thank you.'

'You're welcome,' Céline replied, relieved that Sophia seemed happier now. 'Have you had a good day?'

'I have, thank you. I met my friend, Olivia, and we went out for a wonderful lunch in Marseillan. We had a feast of *coquillage*, the oysters and mussels are hauled up from the Étang *de Thau* and are delivered straight onto the plate within hours.' She licked her lips. 'What a treat.'

'That sounds amazing. I love oysters. Were they raw or cooked?'

'We had both. Raw oysters with lemon and cooked oysters with melted cheese, breadcrumbs and a dash of Noilly Prat. If you like seafood, Céline, we should go together one day.'

Céline beamed. 'I would like that very much.'

The dark atmosphere of the last couple of days had vanished. Sophia seemed to be making every effort to be friendly. 'Shall I give you a tour of the vineyard? It's a pleasant evening and Pascal won't be back from the field for hours.'

'That would be fantastic. Now that I'm staying for a while, it would be helpful to find my bearings. I'll just go and put my boots on.'

Before long the two women made their way from the old house, up the path leading to the entrance of the vineyard. 'So, how are you settling in?'

'My room is comfortable, and I feel very lucky to be able to stay here a while longer.' She hesitated. 'I enjoyed the harvest party, Sophia. What a great celebration it was.'

The corners of Sophia's mouth twitched into a smile. 'It was a good evening, wasn't it? Pascal and I always enjoy rewarding the workers for their hard labour over the year and entertaining our neighbours and competitors.'

Céline furtively glanced towards the outhouse to one side of them. The faded-green door was swinging gently on its hinges.

'The workers like to meet here after work for a drink and a chat. I'm surprised the door has been left open though, perhaps one of the workers is having a nap,' she said, her eyes lingering on the entrance to the stone building.

Lapsing into silence, they walked on to the path following the northern edge of the vines. 'Now that the grapes have been gathered in, the workers are busy preparing the ground for the cold months ahead. They pile up the earth around the vine roots to protect them from the cold and frost.'

'So the soil acts rather like a blanket?'

'Exactly... Most of the grapes have been picked ready to make into wine, but as we pass the top of this field, you'll notice that some grapes have been left on the vine.'

'Why?'

'The longer you leave the grapes to ripen, the sweeter they will become, and so the wine from the late harvest is sweet.'

Céline gazed across the endless rows of vines, ablaze with colour: deep red, bright yellow, and burnished orange. 'The vines are breathtaking, I've never seen anything like them before, they are simply stunning.'

'I know,' Sophia gushed. 'Autumn is my favourite time of the year.'

At the far end of the field, they arrived at a settlement of dwellings, some made of stone and some wooden. 'This is where the workers live. The shacks are simple but comfortable enough for their needs.'

Céline's eyes alighted on a large stone-built house with a red terracotta-tiled roof, some distance from the other accommodation. This double-storey dwelling looked considerably more luxurious, with a mass of vines meandering up the front wall. 'Who lives here?'

'It is Luca's villa. I had it built especially for him a few years ago. He's always been such a conscientious worker and he devotes much of his time to tending the vines. His family, going back generations, have always worked on the land. Luca has an extraordinary knowledge and understanding of how to look after the vines, and he shares his expertise with the other workers.' Her face softened. 'He deserves to live in comfort.'

'You obviously have a hard-working team.'

'But Luca isn't like the others. He is a creature of the land,' she said. 'A wild animal.'

Chapter 14

Something was different. She scanned the surface of the chest of drawers. Something wasn't quite as she had left it. She opened each drawer in turn, but her clothes were untouched. The computer was where she had left it. Her heart beat faster as she checked the whereabouts of her all-important ID document in her desk drawer. It was there, but she was sure that she had stored it more securely; it was lying loosely on top of her other important paperwork. She quickly drew back the rug and looked under the floorboard. Nothing had been disturbed. Puzzled, she felt sure someone had rummaged through her things. Or had she just imagined it?

Pushing worrying thoughts to the back of her mind, Céline decided to go for a walk. She had finished her domestic chores, and she had a couple of hours to herself. This morning, the house was deserted. Pascal had left for work and Sophia was nowhere to be seen. As she walked towards the vineyard, a cold chill seeped through her flimsy jacket, sending a deep shiver down her spine. She quickened her step, her breath condensing in the cold air. She gazed towards the vineyard; the workers would have to work fast to heap the earth round the vine roots before the first frosts of winter.

Suddenly, a figure loomed in front of her, blocking the pathway ahead, casting a deep shadow across her face. He took her roughly by the hand and pulled her into the stone outhouse, closing the door behind him. Pinning her against the uneven stone wall, he grabbed handfuls of hair in each hand. His mouth came down forcefully on hers. Céline's breath became shallow, her body trembling with fear and excitement. He swept over the bare flesh of her collarbones, before crushing her breasts beneath his calloused hands.

Why aren't I screaming for help? Her legs had turned to jelly. *What gives him the right to do this?*

He stripped off her jacket and forced his hands under her dress. She didn't resist; she found herself encouraging him. *Is this what I really want?* He pulled her dress deftly over her hips and, with one swift movement, ripped off her underwear. He knelt in front of her, grasped her buttocks, and pulled her hungrily towards him. Tingles of excitement coursed up and down her spine as he pleasured her. She cried out as powerful pulsating sparks surged through her body. He pulled himself up to full height, engulfing her in his arms, and entered her, taking his pleasure, holding her tightly until his excitement subsided. She shuddered in his arms. There was no finesse; he had been driven to mate, like a wild creature. She caught her breath and stared into his piercingly black eyes. They were crazed; they held little emotion. All of a sudden, his face softened as he brushed his lips across her cheek. And then he was gone.

Céline slumped into the chair, staring unblinkingly into the semi-darkness. She felt shocked but strangely exhilarated by what had just happened. As she inhaled, she could still sense his natural musky scent and his hands rough on her bare skin. He needed no words, he was skilled and masterful. He showed little emotion, just raw desire. But there was something about the expression on his face, just before he left, that surprised her. She saw the merest hint of a smile.

She covered her face with her hands. Had she wanted to have sex with Luca, or had he taken advantage of her against her will? Had he raped her? She swept several damp strands of hair from her face and stared into the gloom. Has she been violated? Should she tell someone? Questions flooded her head. Perhaps she would confide in Pascal, or maybe the old gentleman at the party who had given her the stark warning about Luca. She flinched as she recalled Gaston describing how his son's behaviour had deteriorated since Luca had become his friend.

Uncovering her face, she stared out of the small grubby window, searching for answers. Her body still tingled with pleasure. Maybe she should accept it for what it was: a single fleeting moment of physical pleasure. Perhaps she had wanted it to happen.

Walking out into the glare of the midday sun, she made her way along the periphery of the field towards the workers' encampment. She was curious to see the conditions in which the workers and their families lived. As she arrived at the first shack she was greeted by a friendly buxom woman in her mid-thirties.

'*Bonjour,*' she said with a broad smile. '*Je m'appelle Nathalie,* I think I saw you at the harvest party. Are you staying at the old house?'

'Hi, yes, I'm staying with Pascal and Sophia, and earning my keep doing a few domestic duties for them. I'm Céline, by the way.' She warmed to Nathalie immediately.

'But your accent is not French, I think? Are you German, or English maybe?'

'I'm from England, but my mother was born and brought up in Marseillan. My father was English.'

Nathalie smiled. 'How I would love to visit England. I would go to Buckingham Palace and see the Changing of the Guard… and go on a red double-decker bus.' Her eyes dulled. 'But it will probably never happen, because we will never have enough money. My husband works hard but we have two hungry mouths to feed. Sammy and Lisa…' She gave a deep-throated laugh. 'They're such hard work, and always hungry!'

'Does your husband work on the vines?'

'Thomas drives the van and takes the wines to local markets and restaurants. He's a real charmer, my husband. He's brilliant at advertising and selling his wares. He could convince you to buy a lame dog if he got the chance, believe you me.'

Céline glanced sideways at Nathalie. She had a beautiful round face with dimples in her cheeks, and one or two laughter lines. She wore a low-cut checked dress, showing her ample chest, drawn into her waist by a thick leather belt. Her hands looked considerably older than her face, probably wrinkled from years of housework, and her nails were caked with dirt. She wore brown boots that were laced and muddy from the fields. Her mousey-brown hair was tied back from her face with a rubber band.

'I guess that's why I married him, the old rogue. I hardly ever see him though. Everyone's so busy here. Have you made any friends?'

'I get on well with Pascal and Sophia... and I've met Luca a couple of times.'

'Oh that Luca, he's a rascal.' She giggled, covering her mouth with her hand. 'I think he's had every woman in the village. He has a reputation for taking advantage of anyone feeling lonely. Mind you, we all have to be careful because Sophia gets very jealous...'

Céline's face clouded over. The last thing she wanted to do was to upset the mistress of the house. 'Tell me more about Luca. Has he got a wife or does he live on his own?'

'He's a loner. He lives in the big villa and largely keeps himself to himself. Except, of course, when he's chasing the women. He speaks a different language, Occitan – a local dialect – so he is difficult to understand. He can sure as hell communicate using his hands and body though!' she said with an evil glint in her eye. 'He's worth his weight in gold here; he knows a huge amount about growing vines, and making wine... and, of course, pleasuring women,' she added, playfully eying Céline up and down.

'Well, thanks for the warning. Why does *madame* get jealous?'

'Now you're asking. You will find out soon enough...'

Céline nodded, thinking that now was not the right time to probe any deeper. And, of course, she already knew.

'Perhaps I could go out in the van with Thomas sometime? I would love to visit Marseillan, where my mother grew up. And see one or two of the local markets. Do you think that would be possible?'

Nathalie linked arms with Céline. 'I'm sure Thomas would be pleased to have some company. That's if you can put up with his endless chattering!' She paused. 'This is our home,' she said, pointing to a tiny rundown dwelling, little more than a shed. 'Would you like a Pastis?'

'That would be lovely.'

The two women sat outside on wooden chairs on a makeshift patio: simple, but with a beautiful view. They hugged their coats tightly around themselves to keep warm; the sun had gone down and the temperature was falling rapidly. 'You'd be surprised how cold it gets in winter here. At dusk, the temperatures plummet under the starriest of night skies. I sometimes wrap myself in a thick woollen blanket and sit outside after the kids have gone to bed and just stare into the universe.'

Céline thought sadly that events in her life had taken over, and she didn't seem to find any time to do something as simple as to appreciate the beauty of the night sky.

'And the peace is a welcome relief from the kids, I can tell you,' she said, raising her eyes to heaven.

'Do your children go to school?'

'Yes, they go to the local school, and they seem to enjoy themselves. I'm not sure how much they learn though.'

'So, Nathalie, what do you do when Thomas is at work and the kids are at school?'

'I have a lot to do, cooking and cleaning.' Her shoulders

slumped. 'It can get very lonely here, but thankfully we have a small close-knit community and we all look out for one another.'

'Are most of the workers married with families?'

'We're a real mix: mostly families, quite a few kids, but there are also some singletons. There are a handful of older folk, grandparents, who look after the kids and generally help out with the daily chores. Sadly, my parents died a few years ago... But Thomas's mum comes to visit us from Carcassonne. Oh dear, she's more trouble than Thomas and the kids put together.' She laughed. 'But her heart's in the right place I suppose.'

Céline breathed in the cold air. 'Something smells absolutely delicious. What is it?'

'I've made Thomas's favourite supper tonight. Have you ever tasted *cassoulet*?'

'Yes, it's one of my favourites.'

'Come with me,' she said, beckoning her towards the kitchen. A huge cast-iron pot sat on the flamed gas ring. She lifted the lid and stirred the steaming mix of beans, sausages, pork and tomatoes. She scooped up a generous mound of stew onto a wooden spoon and blew on it to cool it down. 'Have a taste...'

Céline closed her eyes as the delicious mouth-watering stew slipped down her throat. 'It is so good,' she said, as she swallowed a piece of sausage.

'This will last us a couple of days. Even though the kids eat huge quantities, it is a large pot, and we eat it with chunks of bread. The kids are out playing with their friends, but they should be home soon. Would you like to join us for supper? You might even meet Thomas too if you're lucky!'

'Oh my goodness, is that the time?' she said, glancing at her watch. 'I really must go, I need to prepare supper for Pascal and Sophia, and I'm late. Another time?'

'But of course! I hope we see a lot of each other,' said Nathalie with a smile. She leant over and kissed Céline on both cheeks. 'À *bientôt*.'

The light was fading rapidly as Céline negotiated the rough pathway back towards the old house. As she glanced to her left she saw, to her surprise, the outline of a woman striding purposefully in the opposite direction. Recognising her immediately, she slunk into the shadows, hoping that she had not been seen. She watched as Sophia made her way towards the large villa at the end of the group of dwellings. Céline pulled her jacket around her and sighed. She still couldn't quite process what had happened with Luca in the outhouse, but she knew she was playing with fire. Sophia must never find out.

'Hello, Céline, have you had a good day?' Pascal was sitting by the kitchen table in the semi-darkness. 'I feel I could sleep for a week.'

'I'm sorry, Pascal, I went out for a walk and the time flew by. I meant to prepare supper for you and Sophia long before now.'

'Don't worry at all. It's just me this evening. Sophia was in one of her strange moods and she's gone for a walk. When she gets like this, nothing I can say will make any difference.' He stared sadly into the distance. 'There's some salad and a *tielle sétoise* in the fridge. We could share it. I shouldn't think you've tasted anything like this before; it is a local delicacy made with tomato sauce, chicken, squid and garlic wrapped in pastry and sprinkled with paprika. Are you hungry?'

Céline realised that she was ravenous, she had had nothing to eat since breakfast. 'It sounds delicious, I'll prepare it now.' She busied herself arranging two inviting plates of pie and salad while Pascal poured a generous measure of *Picpoul de Pinet* into two crystal wine glasses. The kitchen felt cold and formal, in stark contrast to the warm and friendly atmosphere of Nathalie's simple dwelling.

'I have just visited the commune up towards the far end of the vineyard. Who lives there?'

'Mostly people who work at the vineyard, but there are also workers from neighbouring vineyards, and I think there are also some folk who work in the local shops and businesses in Marseillan. The accommodation isn't very comfortable, but most of the community seem content, and, if they work hard, they earn a reasonable salary.'

He suddenly turned towards Céline and put his arm around her shoulder. 'Sophia is often out these days, and I spend many long evenings alone. I'm so glad you're here, you bring light into my life.'

Chapter 15

22 February 1943

My head holds horrific images of what I left behind. The agony on their faces will live with me forever. Their eyes express astonishment, isolation, fear, their mouths open in silent terror. Death and destruction, and all for what? Between 22 and 24 January 1943, the German army, supported by the French police, rounded up the Jews and the immigrant population of the Old Port. They were taken from their homes and their businesses and transported on a train to Hell. Whole streets and districts bombed to the ground. Generations of families destroyed in the blink of an eye. My heart aches with sadness.

When Beth's uncle warned me of the Vichy intention, I left Marseille under the cover of darkness, walked for miles, and eventually flagged down a lorry carrying a cargo of wine. The driver was sympathetic to my plight and offered to take me away from immediate danger. He drove me to a vineyard near Marseillan and dropped me at the entrance, advising me to ask if there was any work I could do on the vines. I am indebted to the driver. I wish I'd asked his name.

Imagine my relief and gratitude when the owner, Monsieur Renaurd, offered me some temporary manual

work. He asked me nothing, saying that the more he knew,
the more he would put himself and his family in danger.

On a clear day, if I stare into the distance I can just see
the rocky snow-capped peaks of the Pyrenees. The weather
is too inclement at the moment to make the hazardous
journey, but my hope is that I can find a guide and, in the
spring, I will walk across the mountains to freedom. And
one day, God willing, I will be reunited with my family and
my darling Beth.

One day.

Céline clutched the journal tightly with both hands until
her finger nails turned white. How Isaac Goldmann
and thousands of other Jews and immigrants must have
suffered, their families torn apart, their homes bombed
to the ground, and the chance of a successful life and
happiness destroyed. She put her head in her hands. How
could it happen? Why?

***

Life had settled into a routine at the vineyard. Céline
always went for her early morning swim at dawn, just as
the sun was rising. Luca was always there, watching and
waiting for her. They would take advantage of the quiet of
the morning to retreat to the line of whispering cypress
trees and explore each other in ways that were new and
exciting. There were few words, but recently she had
noticed a subtle change in Luca. His eyes held emotion:
affection, even. His touch was tender as his hands glided

smoothly and expertly following the curves of her body. He had the power to make Céline feel attractive and desirable, but she also felt strangely unnerved by his emotions that had begun to rise to the surface. Now she could see an unmistakable pool of love in his dark eyes, and she was not sure that this was what she wanted. Life was complicated enough already, and she felt the need to remain detached and focussed. She knew she was living a lie and, at some point, she would have to face her demons. But not yet. It was imperative that she did not give too much of herself away.

At first she found sex with Luca a welcome physical release, an uncomplicated arrangement that was purely about sex: just sex. She was surprised to find that she could now separate sex from emotion; she enjoyed sex in its own right, rather like a sport. Once emotions become involved – love, affection, anger, jealousy – everything becomes more complicated. She could have sex without love or, conversely, she could have love without sex. One was not dependent on the other. She realised that her new discovery was immensely liberating; she felt powerful and in control. But was it all about to change?

Did Sophia know about the relationship that she had with Luca? Céline wasn't sure, but she had noticed that Sophia had become increasingly cold and cutting in her comments. 'Look at the state of the kitchen surfaces, were you brought up in a barn?' Céline always muttered her apologies and worked tirelessly to fulfil Sophia's increasingly demanding expectations. Her manner was different when Pascal came home from work. Sophia was sugary and sweet with Céline, skilful at hiding her true feelings. Pascal seemed oblivious to the increasingly tense atmosphere between the two women. She would whisper sweet nothings into Pascal's ear and then she would leave, always making an excuse: she needed fresh air, or she needed time to herself. But Céline knew exactly where she was going.

Pascal and Céline were left alone, another familiar feature in the daily routine. He gazed at her, his head full of questions. Every morning he opened the curtains to the bedroom and he took guilty pleasure in watching Céline unwrap her dressing gown and bare her naked body to the chill of the dawn. He loved to watch her glide effortlessly through the water, swimming length after length, despite the cold winds blowing from the mountains. But then after her swim, she would simply disappear. He was puzzled, always checking that she wasn't walking on the pathway leading back to the old house. The chickens roamed, clucking cheerfully, but there was never any sign of Céline returning for at least half an hour, every day. Where did she go at that time? What did she do?

'How's the swimming going, Céline? It must be getting colder now that the winter is approaching.' He scratched his head. 'I suppose it must take a long time for the water to cool down, and the solar heating will top up the temperature on a sunny day. Do you put the cover on every time you finish your swim?'

'I don't always remember, thanks for reminding me. I'm usually in a hurry to get back into the warm and put some clothes on.'

Pascal looked at her searchingly. 'Do you ever go for a jog around the field afterwards?'

Céline giggled. 'You'll never find me going for a run!'

She suddenly tensed, aware that the pool was overlooked by Pascal and Sophia's bedroom. Maybe he had noticed her leaving the swimming pool and heading for the row of cypress trees. They would have to be more careful and arrange an alternative meeting place and time, well away from the all-seeing eyes of Sophia.

'Would you mind me joining you occasionally for an early morning swim? I have a little more time now that autumn is here.'

'Of course not, Pascal.'

'Great, although I'm not sure how much longer we can do this for now that the weather is changing.'

Pascal sat quietly in his chair. His pale skin fascinated her; it looked so fresh and clean, almost luminous in the fading light. She found him surprisingly attractive; his body reminded her of a marble sculpture that she had at once seen at the Victoria & Albert Museum. But there was an air of sadness about him and Céline wondered how much he knew about Sophia's evening exploits. She resolved to find ways of cheering him up; she was becoming very fond of him. He was a kind, generous and sensitive soul and he deserved more.

'I think I'm off to bed, I've got an early start in the fields tomorrow,' he said, interrupting her train of thought. 'But first, would you like a nightcap? I've got a special bottle of Armagnac in the cupboard. I think I'm going to have one.'

'Oh, yes please, that would be a lovely way to end the day.'

As the smooth liquid trickled down her throat, warm and comforting, she felt a wave of contentment wash over her, relaxing in a way that she had been unable to do in her past life in Oxford all those months ago.

As Pascal stood up to leave, his hand lingered on her shoulder, and he moved towards her and kissed her lightly on both cheeks. 'À *demain, ma chérie. Bonne nuit.*'

Céline was left alone with her thoughts. She could feel genuine warmth and affection between her and Pascal. Although they hadn't known each other for long, there seemed to be a connection between them, a sensitivity and understanding that she would cherish as something precious in life. She hoped their growing friendship wouldn't antagonise Sophia further.

Over the last couple of weeks, she had enjoyed getting to know Nathalie, the wife of one of the workers; she was easy to talk to and Céline could relax with her. She was a hard-working mother of two young children. Humble, with a heart of gold. Céline didn't know her well enough yet to be sure, but her gut feeling told her that Nathalie would become a very good friend. She had invited Céline to a street party the following evening and she was looking forward to it. She decided it wouldn't be wise to share this with Sophia and Pascal; after all, what she did in her own time was her business.

The image of Sophia, her dark eyes glinting with anger, dominated her dreams, merging with the terror of her deceased husband's demise. When the first light of the morning seeped through the cracks in the shutters, she peeled herself out of bed and threw on her dressing gown. Although she enjoyed her early morning swim, it was sometimes a struggle to find the energy and enthusiasm. The chickens seemed to wait for her and clucked merrily around her feet as she followed the now-familiar path to the swimming pool. As she edged herself into the water, a chill took her breath away. The temperature of the air and the water was now considerably colder than it had been, and she wondered how much longer she would take regular swims.

'*Salut*,' Pascal said cheerily, as he slid into the water. 'I'm going to be busy later, but I think a quick swim will energise me for the long day ahead.'

Céline glanced around furtively. She hadn't had time to agree to a new time and place with Luca, and she hoped that he would be discreet. 'What's happening at work today?'

'I have a meeting with my suppliers, and it tends to be very long and laborious. I shall be glad when it's all over. In the afternoon I'm meeting with Gaston to pick his brains about one or two new ideas he has to promote the vineyard. He's a wise old gentleman. Yes, rather old-fashioned, but sometimes there's a lot to be said for less-modern practices.'

'Ah yes, I met Gaston at the harvest party. I enjoyed our conversation, he seemed really interesting and wise. I would love to see him again.' She recalled how he had confided in her about the concern he had about Pierre, his son, who had become withdrawn since he had struck up a friendship with Luca.

'Gaston always welcomes visitors. I'm sure he would be delighted to see you anytime. He lives just beyond the hedge over there,' he said, lifting his arm out of the water and pointing to the cypress trees. 'Oh look, there's Luca now. He must be collecting the milk. He never seems to sleep, that boy!'

Céline jerked her head, breathing in a large mouthful of cold water. She caught a glimpse of Luca's long hair shining in the sunlight as he hurried in the opposite direction. Struggling to catch her breath, Pascal strode towards her and thumped her on the back until her coughing fit subsided.

'I'm sorry, I didn't mean to hurt you, Céline,' he said, stroking her back gently. 'Are you okay?'

'I'm fine, thanks.' She was annoyed with herself that she had made such a drama out of something that she should have played down. Of course, Luca often came in the early morning to collect the milk. So why should Pascal suspect anything?

At that moment, she turned to see Sophia at the gate, silent and still, her eyes darting from one to the other.

Chapter 16

Sparks from the orange flames danced upwards into the cold night air. Céline perched on a low three-legged wooden stool and gazed around her. It was Saturday evening at the workers' commune and the atmosphere was alive with conversation and laughter. Boisterous children weaved in and out of the people gathering around the fire pit, squealing with pleasure. How different it was to the rather formal atmosphere in the old house. Here, Céline could breathe in the convivial atmosphere: everyone was having fun and enjoying the company of others.

'How are you doing, Céline? You should grab some *coq au vin* before it all goes. I make huge quantities, and it always disappears in a flash. Come on,' Nathalie said, grabbing Céline's hand and propelling her into the kitchen. A cast-iron pan, now half-full, bubbled on the hob. Céline ladled herself a generous portion of chicken, inhaling the delicious aroma, and settled herself on an upturned crate close to the fire pit. Her friend pulled up a stool beside her. 'It must be rather overwhelming for you not knowing many people here. And everyone is speaking French.'

'I don't mind at all, I'm just soaking up the atmosphere. Everyone seems to be having a great time,'

Céline said, glancing around her. 'How often do you have get-togethers like this?'

'Oh, it's hard to say. We tend to get together more when there is less work for the workers on the vines.' Nathalie giggled. 'I guess our social gatherings ebb and flow with the seasons, but we have them as often as we can. After all, everyone enjoys a good party. I must go and serve up supper for the kids. Help yourself to a glass of wine,' she said as she bustled into the throng of people.

'*Bonsoir, madame.* I think I saw you at the harvest party.'

Céline looked up to see an elderly gentleman, stooping over his walking stick, peering down at her. 'Yes, I remember you, Gaston,' she said, grateful to see a familiar face. 'Come and join me.' She drew up a high-backed wooden chair.

'I shall be glad to rest my weary legs. I'm afraid I've forgotten your name, my memory is terrible these days,' he said, looking at her, his pale-blue eyes, dull with age.

'Don't worry, Gaston, I can be very forgetful too. I'm Céline. It's a lovely evening isn't it?'

'Ah yes, Céline… a very beautiful name. Tell me, how are you enjoying life at the old house?'

Céline considered her answer carefully. 'Everything is going well I think, but you would have to ask Pascal and Sophia to see if they agree with me. I'm grateful they have welcomed me into their home, and I try to keep the house tidy and prepare some tasty meals. Mind you, I don't think my cooking is up to Nathalie's standard,' she said, taking a large mouthful of casserole. 'I shall have to ask her for a few recipes.'

'How do you find Sophia? She is a little volatile, yes?' He raised his eyebrows. 'Pascal is the salt of the earth, but Sophia…' His words faded into the distance, and silence descended between them. 'She is beautiful, but she has a cruel edge to her.'

'And what about you, Gaston? How is your son?' She swallowed, not wishing to engage in conversation about Sophia, but immediately regretting her direct question regarding his ailing son.

The old man hunched his shoulders, his face creased in despair. 'Pierre is not good, I'm really worried about him. He doesn't go out anymore, he just stays in his room for hours on end, only appearing for meals. But then he doesn't eat,' he said, drawing his arthritic fingers roughly through his hair. 'I'm at my wits' end. I don't know what to do.'

'I'm so sorry. Hopefully he'll get through this. Time is a great healer.'

He stared vacantly, longing to believe the words she uttered. 'If only he hadn't met Luca, things might have been very different…'

Céline remained motionless, absorbing everything that Gaston had expressed. 'I do hope Pierre feels brighter soon,' she said, putting her arm around his shoulder. 'If there is anything I can do to help, let me know.'

His back straightened. 'There is one thing. Would you come for tea with me one afternoon next week? Wednesday? I think it might help Pierre to meet you, and it would certainly cheer me up too. You would be like a breath of fresh air.'

'Of course, I would be delighted. Pascal has told me where you live, and Wednesday afternoon would suit me well.'

His face broke into a smile. 'Shall we say four o'clock?'

'Perfect.'

Gaston peered at his watch. 'It's time I went home.' He smiled again and squeezed her hands in his. 'I can't thank you enough.' He slowly and painfully rose to standing and stumbled away, leaving Céline wondering if she had been wise to agree to his invitation. She was not confident that she could lift Pierre out of the doldrums, but she would do her best for Gaston.

'Ah, there you are. I want you to meet my husband, Thomas.'

Céline glanced from Nathalie to Thomas. Her eyes drifted upwards from his torso to his face; he was probably the tallest man she had ever met. He had a round friendly face with twinkling eyes and messy blond hair. He shook her hand with a crushing grip. 'Nat has told me a lot about you. It isn't all true, is it?' He threw back his head and erupted into peals of laughter.

'Oh, Thomas, behave,' Nathalie chastised. Turning to Céline she whispered, 'He's a gentle giant, just remember to take most of what he says with a pinch of salt.' Nathalie looked up at her husband with almost tangible love in her eyes. 'I can't take you anywhere.'

'So, tell me, Céline, what brings you to this beautiful part of France?'

'It's a long story and I won't bore you with it. Safe to say, I travelled from England a few weeks ago and I'm earning my keep doing some domestic duties up at the old house.'

'Well, I admire you. It is a brave thing to up-sticks, leave your homeland behind and explore a foreign land. Are you travelling alone?'

'Yes, I am. I enjoy my own company, and I'm free to do exactly what I want.' She averted her gaze. If he knew the truth about why she had been forced to leave England, he might not have so much respect for her.

'Sounds great to me. I remember those halcyon days when I had no responsibilities – surfing, drinking, free love – but now I wouldn't swap my Nat or the kids for anything on earth.' He cocked his head to one side and winked. 'Except maybe—'

'Céline has asked if she can come with you in the van one day when you are delivering, so that she can see more of Marseillan and the surrounding villages,' Nathalie interrupted.

'Of course! I would be pleased to have some company. I'll give you the full tour and lunch, but I'm afraid it might involve eating a few oysters and drinking a glass or two of Chardonnay.' He smiled, revealing his startlingly irregular teeth. 'There's no time like the present. How about tomorrow morning? I usually head off in the van at about six-thirty.'

Céline beamed from ear to ear. 'I would like that very much… and I adore oysters. It's a date.' She had immediately warmed to Thomas. He seemed friendly with a wicked sense of humour. She would look forward to the day ahead.

'I'll meet you outside the main gate.' He turned towards Nathalie and engulfed her in his arms. 'Come on, *ma chérie*, we need to put those little rascals to bed.' He reached into his bag and pulled out a bottle of wine. 'Here's a bottle of last year's vintage that I think you might enjoy, a present from me to you. See you tomorrow, bright and early.'

After having said her farewells, she wandered back to the old house, clutching her gift. She felt slightly tipsy but elated from the evening and the unconditional welcome she had received from these friendly folk.

Quietly opening the door, she tripped on the step and noisily fastened the ancient cast-iron latch behind her, the sound echoing in the darkness. Hearing a chuckle, she peaked round the kitchen door to find Pascal surrounded by a sea of paperwork.

'That was quite an entrance, Céline, it must have been a *good* evening.' He smirked.

'Oh dear, I'm sorry, Pascal. I'm glad I didn't wake you. Nathalie invited me to a party at the workers' commune, and the hospitality was so warm and welcoming, I found it hard to tear myself away. What have you been up to?'

'Nothing much, just catching up with some rather tedious admin. Sophia is out on another of her night-time jaunts. She's told me not to wait up so I thought it was a good opportunity to catch up with some work.'

'I've just been given a rather special bottle of wine by Thomas, would you like a glass?'

'Ah, from Thomas, that should be pretty good.'

She reached into the drawer and pulled out a corkscrew.

'I'll get some glasses,' Pascal said, his face radiating pleasure.

Céline clumsily poured the wine, spilling a few drops which formed red rings around the base of each glass, soaking quickly into the soft wood of the table. 'Whoops, I'd never make a sommelier!'

'*Santé!*' Pascal said, turning to Céline. 'Here's to us.' He paused to take a sip. 'It's not bad. It needs more time to breathe, and maybe another couple of years in the bottle, but it's quite drinkable.'

She glanced at Pascal, fascinated by the way the pupils of his eyes flickered, oscillating within his eye sockets. He seemed to be looking at her, but she couldn't be sure. He tenderly placed his soft warm hand on her shoulder. 'You are one of the most strong and beautiful women I have ever met, Céline.' He pulled her gently towards him, so close that she could feel his warm breath on her neck. He planted a kiss on her cheek.

She leaned across and kissed him, their lips meeting passionately. Céline melted into his arms, enjoying his firm but tender embrace as she listened to the rhythmic sound of his heart pounding in his chest. Suddenly, she caught her breath and pulled back. 'I'm sorry, Pascal…'

'Please don't apologise, it's one of the most exciting things that's happened to me for a long time,' he said softly.

'But what about Sophia?'

He shook his head. 'She's lost interest in me. We still love each other, but the physical side of our relationship died a long time ago.'

'Ah, I'm sorry,' she said, thinking to herself how lucky Sophia was to have such a caring husband. 'We humans can be complicated; there is often no rhyme or reason for our behaviour. But Jacques and Nicole made me realise that we must seize the day and enjoy what we can. Life is short.'

'I'm very fond of those two, and they are right.'

They kissed again, more passionately this time, one of his hands encircling her waist, the other tenderly holding her hand. Céline stood up and gently propelled him towards the stairs.

'Are you sure, Céline?'

She silently led the way to her dimly lit bedroom. The time passed in a haze of warmth, pleasure and tenderness.

Towards dawn, the spell was broken abruptly by the loud click of the latch lifting on the front door. They froze, the sound of her footsteps climbing the stairs resonating in their ears. All of a sudden, the antiquated water system clunked into action as Sophia turned on the shower.

'I must go,' he whispered urgently.

'Sleep well, Pascal... And no regrets.'

Chapter 17

It was mid-morning and they had already made several deliveries to rural village stores on the way to Marseillan. Each visit involved lively banter, raucous laughter and *la bise*. French was spoken at a lightning-quick speed and Céline struggled to understand some of the conversation. Numerous crates of wine and money were exchanged and everyone seemed delighted.

As they drove through the narrow treelined streets of Marseillan, Céline admired the typically French architecture: two- and three-storey stone-built terraced houses, boasting elegant wrought-iron Juliette balconies and large ornate doors opening straight out onto the pavement. The town was an interesting mix of commercial and residential properties; a shop selling seafood adjacent to a row of residential terraces; a hairdresser next to a small commercial garage.

It was approaching midday, siesta time, and the streets were fairly quiet except for a few people going about their daily business. Thomas negotiated the narrow streets, driving perilously close to the wing mirrors of cars parked on either side of the road; he must have known the width of his van to the nearest centimetre. Eventually, they arrived at a small port. Thomas followed the water's edge, finally drawing up in front of a line of primitive shacks, all with corrugated roofs, proudly displaying rusty signs advertising their produce. The van came to a standstill beside an incongruous gathering of prestige cars: Porsches, Mercedes and Range Rovers.

'These people are very discerning and know where to come for a good lunch,' Thomas explained. 'They serve the best shellfish this region has to offer. The oysters win national awards. Let's go to the café over there, Céline. They know me well, and we will have very good service.'

As Céline jumped out of the van, she wrinkled her nose; the overpowering smell of oyster and mussel shells, discarded in huge crates at the roadside, was quite unpleasant. As they opened the door, Thomas was welcomed like an old friend. They paused to admire the oysters and mussels stored in deep tanks to one side, available for customers to select and take away. The restaurant itself opened out to an outdoor area adorned with fishing nets, fairy lights and lanterns. An open fire blazed in one corner. '*Tu vas bien, Thomas?*' a friendly waitress asked, as she led them to a small metal table next to the water.

'*Oui*, ça *va*, ça *va*,' Thomas replied cheerily.

The ground to one side of the restaurant was piled high with thick chains, haulage equipment, tangled fishing nets, containers of all shapes and sizes and old rusty bicycles. The calm water in front of them, dotted with fishing boats, stretched out as far as the eye could see; green turning to blue in the distance, reflecting the pale-blue autumnal sky.

Céline had never seen anything like this: a perfect juxtaposition of industry and indulgence. Fishermen hauled in their catch at regular intervals, and proud members of staff served delicious shellfish, straight from the Étang *de Thau* onto the plate.

Thomas ordered a small bottle of Chardonnay, produced by a local winery, and a selection of raw and cooked oysters and mussels followed by a *Brasucade*. 'Prepare for a feast, Céline.'

At that moment, the waitress produced two small glasses of Noilly Prat, a local aperitif. 'On the house,' she said with a warm smile.

Thomas nodded his thanks. 'Now, Céline, tell me more about yourself. You speak good French – not perfect, but good enough.' He laughed. 'Did you learn the language at school?'

'Yes, I learnt some of the basics at school, but my mother was born and brought up here in Marseillan.'

'Well, fancy that,' he said, raising his eyebrows.

'I was bilingual as a child, but I'm afraid my French is a bit rusty now.'

'Um. Not quite as rusty as my English.'

'My mother always talked fondly of her French upbringing, but then she fell madly in love with my dad, an English man through and through, and she lived in England for the rest of her life. Since she died, I have felt the need to explore this area, it helps me to feel close to her. Does that sound crazy?'

'Not at all. Do you know where she lived?'

'Yes, I have an address. I wonder if her family house still exists…'

'Perhaps we could take a detour after lunch and find out.'

Céline's eyes lit up. 'I would love that, Thomas, but only if you have time?'

'Of course, it would be interesting for me too.'

At that moment, the waitress produced an ice bucket containing a small bottle of white wine. Thomas poured the cold liquid into two glasses. '*Santé*! I hope you're enjoying your day, Céline. After lunch, I would like to pop into Chez Madeleine,' he said, pointing to his glass. 'This wine was produced there, and then we will go and search out your mother's house.'

The restaurant was quickly filling up with smartly dressed couples and families with young children all enjoying lively conversation and delicious food. Glancing round, Céline was impressed with the behaviour of the children, who seemed fully engaged and immersed in conversation.

The oyster and mussel platters were served on large plastic plates and presented meticulously, each shell favoured with different ingredients: raw oysters with tomato and tabasco and cooked oysters marinated in Noilly Prat and topped with melted cheese, crispy at the edges. Céline had never tasted raw mussels before but they slipped down her throat easily with a mouth-watering burst of the Étang *de Thau*. Her eyes were drawn to the open fire blazing under a large steel pan laden with glistening mussels.

'That is the *Brasucade*. Mussels are cooked over burning vine roots and served in a rich sauce, flavoured with tomatoes and spices. The vine roots give them a slightly smoky flavour.'

White smoke curled upwards from the fire and the ruddy-faced chef stirred the mussels noisily and enthusiastically with a large spoon before tossing large helpings into enamelled pots. Céline watched, fascinated by the attention to detail and the pride of all serving this very special local fare. The emphasis was placed on serving top-quality food and wine, rather than providing a luxurious environment, leather-backed chairs and chandeliers. This setting was exquisite in its simplicity.

'What made you decide to come to France, apart from exploring your mother's origins, Céline?'

Her face reddened. 'Things had become rather complicated at home and so I decided to take the plunge, leave everything behind, and explore new pastures.'

'Forgive me if I am prying, but are you running away from something? Your expression is telling me a story.'

Céline wished, not for the first time, that her face didn't give so much away about her inner feelings.

'I suppose I am in a way. Life hasn't always been easy, I've been through some very dark times.' She shrugged her shoulders. 'But we can't expect to breeze through life without a few skirmishes along the way, can we? I'm glad I left when I did though, and I am enjoying my new adventures in France.'

Thomas sensed that Céline was not keen to pursue the conversation any further. 'Well, I've certainly had my ups and downs, but I think it is living the ups and surviving the downs that make us into who we are.'

Nibbling the cheese from the outer shell of one of her oysters, she marvelled at the insight and understanding that Thomas was showing her. 'Now, tell me about you.'

Thomas took a deep breath. 'Well, there's not really much to tell. I spent much of my misspent youth playing with my friends in the fields and generally getting up to mischief, and then I met Nat.' He stared dreamily into the distance. 'She's my soulmate... And then we had the little ruffians, and life has never been the same again.' He looked at Céline with a twinkle in his eye. 'It's much better, of course, but they drive me mad sometimes. I wouldn't do without them though!'

'And what about your work?'

'I've been a driver for the vineyard for years. Pascal is a great boss and a good friend. I love my job. I meet interesting people, and I get to do things like this,' he said, waving his arm extravagantly across the table. 'I followed in my father's footsteps. He was a driver in this region during the war. *Papa* was a good man with a heart of gold. He helped hundreds of marginalised people, persecuted during the war: Jews, immigrants and underprivileged minorities. He knew trustworthy guides who would take them over the Pyrenees to Spain. *Papa* would drop them off at the foothills, risking his own life, where they would be looked after by a network of people who helped escapees, fleeing occupied France. I think the escape route was also used by allied airmen who had been shot down.'

Silence descended as Céline processed what Thomas had just told her.

'Did he help people to escape the round-up of the Jews in Marseille in 1943?'

'Yes, he did. He used to stow them in the back of his van after dark. Why do you ask?'

Her mind turned to Mr Isaac Goldmann and how he was safely delivered to the vineyard all those years ago. Could the driver who helped Isaac escape be Thomas's father? She furrowed her brow, deep in thought. 'Do you know, Thomas, I have something that you might be very interested in reading.'

'I'm intrigued, tell me more.'

'I've found a journal that I think might be of historical interest. I'm in the middle of translating the diary of a Jewish man who escaped persecution in Marseille in 1943, and he was taken to the vineyard by a local van driver.'

Thomas stared at her in astonishment. '*Vraiment*? Where did you find this journal?'

Céline paused, nervous about giving too much away about how she had unearthed her discovery. 'I would like to finish the translation, it shouldn't take me long, and then let's meet and I will tell you the whole story.'

'I can hardly wait, I wonder if it was *Papa*. There weren't many people during that time who were prepared to put their own lives in peril to save others, and the Nazis were ruthless in punishing anyone who went against them.' He rubbed his face with his hands. 'If I am half the man he was, I would be happy. Did the gentleman mention the name of the driver?'

Céline shook her head sadly. 'No, I'm afraid Isaac didn't ask his name.'

'Perhaps we will never know,' he said sadly.

'I have only translated a few random entries from a detailed diary. An expert more versed in the language and the history during that time will certainly uncover more detail. You never know, Isaac might have had further encounters with the driver. We might yet find out who this brave hero was.'

Thomas's face broke into a wide smile. 'What a find! I look forward to reading it, whether it is my father or not.'

The empty plates were cleared away and two black enamel pots were placed in front of them. Thomas opened the lid with glee to reveal a huge mountain of mussels gleaming in a buttery sauce and sprinkled with parsley. He placed the upturned lid beside the pot and sighed with contentment. He plucked the first mussel with his fingers, and then used the empty shell as a pincer to prise out the flesh from the other shells, discarding the empties in the lid. His movements were swift and skilful as he focussed on the feast in front of him. Céline tried to copy his technique but she was not quite as adept. Within minutes his bowl was empty and the lid was brimming over with discarded shells. Her bowl was still half full.

'I can't eat another morsel.' She sighed, wiping her mouth with her serviette. 'What an amazing lunch. I don't think I'll need any supper tonight.'

He pulled her bowl towards him. 'I hate to see good food go to waste.' He polished off the remaining mussels and licked his lips. 'Let's have a coffee and plan our afternoon. Where did your mother live as a child?'

Céline grasped a small notebook from her handbag, licked her index finger and turned several pages. 'Ah, here it is – 44 Rue 11 Novembre. Do you know where it is?'

'It's just round the corner from here. It would make sense to go to Chez Madeleine first, and then the road you mention is the second turning on the right on our way back to the vineyard.'

'That sounds wonderful.' She turned her gaze once again to the Étang *de Thau*. One or two fishing boats were bobbing about on the rippled water, and high above them, gulls soared effortlessly in the air, their wings outstretched and motionless. On the edge of the inlet, a heron stood stock-still waiting for a fish to come into the range of his powerful beak.

'Chez Madeleine is another local winery, I know the family well. They have gradually expanded their vineyard over the last fifty years. Madeleine produces a very powerful red wine, matured in new oak casks. We winemakers like to compare notes and sample other local wines. I'm sure we will exchange a case or two of our finest wines. Although we are competitors, we all strive for excellence.'

The winery looked like a rather shabby warehouse from the outside, Inconspicuous, with large areas of flaking paintwork. The three-storey building was tall enough to house several huge stainless-steel tanks, which contained the fermenting wine.

As they opened the heavy wooden door, the bell sounded to signal their arrival. Céline blinked as her eyes became accustomed to the dim lighting of the long hall. Large oak barrels lined one side, and dozens of cases of wine nestled in alcoves in the deep stone wall on the other. Boxed wines, generally cheaper, were piled high against the back wall. And cheaper still, were available from what looked like petrol pumps, where customers decanted wine into their own containers, sometimes as big as oil drums.

A few customers milled around, pulling large trolleys, assessing what they should buy. Conversations were muted; there was a hushed atmosphere, reminding Céline of the ancient village churches she used to visit as a child with her parents. It seemed fitting to liken the winery with a church; after all, the art of winemaking commands respect, and is like a religion.

At the far end stood a wooden table, on which were wine glasses ready for customers to taste the wine before buying it. A tempting list displayed the varieties and prices on offer. The wines for tasting were kept in a tall wine fridge so that the customers could enjoy them at their optimum temperatures.

'*Bonjour, Thomas.* Where have you been? We haven't seen you for ages,' the owner's daughter chastised. 'How's Nathalie and those gorgeous children?'

Thomas raised an eyebrow. '"Gorgeous?" I'm not sure about that.' He grinned. 'They're as lively as ever, and Nat is fine, thanks. How's that handsome man of yours?'

'He never stops working, but business is thriving. And who is this?' she asked.

'*Elle s'appelle* Céline. She comes from England and is working up at the old house to earn her keep.' Turning to Céline, he added, 'This is my good friend, Brigette.'

The two women smiled warmly.

'Ah, you're from England. What do you think about Brexit? A bloody disaster, that's what I hear.'

'What's done is done, and we have to live with the consequences… But who knows what the future may bring,' she added optimistically.

'I'm afraid this is just a quick visit,' Thomas interjected. 'Shall we swap a few bottles while I'm here? You might like to sample our new blend that Luca has been working on. I've got six bottles in the van.'

'Of course, Thomas,' she said, reaching for one of the cases of *Père Joseph*. 'We have sold more cases of this than any other, and it is one of our more expensive wines. And yes, of course, we would love to sample a drop of Château Pascal, especially if Luca has had a hand in the making. He's very skilful.'

Céline smiled, pleased to hear that Luca was complimented on his work.

After exchanging the wine, they said their fond farewells and hopped back into the van.

'À *bientôt, j'espère*,' Brigette called, her words fading into the distance.

As the van pulled up outside 44 Rue 11 Novembre, Céline saw a simple dwelling; it was old but looked as if it had been well looked after over the years. It was a stone-built house, with shutters cheerily painted in red, matching the brightly painted front door. White sheets billowed on the washing line like a yacht running under full sail. Two young children, a boy and a girl, screamed with pleasure as they darted in and out of the washing, leaving muddy handprints in their wake. Céline slowly climbed out of the van and studied the scene in front of her. She imagined her mother living here, many years before. Perhaps she had enjoyed playing in the garden, just as these children were now.

'It looks like a happy house, doesn't it?'

'It does... It really does,' she agreed. 'My mother was proud of her French heritage, and she enjoyed a happy childhood here. I know a house is only bricks and mortar, but this house radiates happiness. I thought I might feel sad and nostalgic, but I don't... I loved my mother with all my heart, I still do, and I like to imagine her living here.'

She looked up to see his expression, full of compassion. 'Grief is a strange emotion, isn't it? I struggled when my papa died, but, after months of pain and tears, I realised that I owed it to him to make something of myself and enjoy my life to the fullest. I will never forget him.'

'I would give anything to see my mother again. But I feel better now that I can visualise the house and the town where she was born and grew up. It has helped me. Thank you, Thomas.'

He engulfed her in a warm hug. 'It's time we went home, Nat will be wondering where I am.'

It had been a wonderful day and, as Céline walked up the path to the old house, she felt rather sad that it was over. She had enjoyed every minute, but now she felt weary and ready for bed. She unlatched the door.

'Céline, come in here now.' Her sharp voice cut through the air like a knife through butter.

She gingerly opened the door to the kitchen to find Sophia sitting bolt upright by the table, her black eyes glinting with anger. 'What is this?'

Céline swallowed nervously.

'Look.' She pointed to two red rings on the surface of the wooden table in front of her. 'Was it you?'

Chapter 18

Heavy clouds swept across the silver-grey sky and she felt gloom descend with the rain that had now started to fall. She knew she must clear the air with Sophia, but she felt angry. How hypocritical to accuse her of doing something as innocent as sharing a drink with Pascal, when she was out having sex with Luca. What would Sophia do if she knew the truth?

She had become fond of Pascal and hated the way Sophia treated him, but she knew he must fight his own battles without her interference. She understood his desire for human contact – with her – but she would not continue to encourage him, but neither would she avoid him. The time they had shared together was enjoyable. He was gentle, kind and attentive. Or perhaps, she wondered, did she just feel sorry for him?

Céline shivered. It was too cold for an early morning swim today. She glanced at her watch. It was eight-thirty, and she had agreed to meet Luca at the outhouse, their new meeting place, at nine. After grabbing some breakfast, she threw on her raincoat and made her way up the path.

When she arrived, the outhouse stood silent and empty. Scanning the field ahead and the path leading back to where she had come, he was nowhere to be seen. It was nine-fifteen; he was late. Céline slumped in the chair and waited. What on earth could have happened? She had become accustomed to her liaisons with Luca, he had become a significant part of her daily routine. When she was with him, she felt a powerful cocktail of ecstasy and dread in equal measure; carnal pleasure, touched with the fear of discovery.

Puzzled, she decided to visit Nathalie to cheer herself up. Following the perimeter of the field, the wind whipped through her coat, sending deep shivers up and down her spine, and the icy raindrops stung her cheeks.

As she approached the workers' commune, everything felt different. All the doors and shutters were closed and bolted, and the street was eerily deserted. Something was wrong. She knocked on the door to Nathalie's shack. There was no answer. She knocked again, louder this time. Her son, pale and gaunt, peered out and opened the door wider to let her in. She found Nathalie sitting with her back to the door, silent, her shoulders shuddering.

'What is it, Nathalie?' she said, rushing to comfort her friend. 'What's happened?'

She lifted her head and stared at Céline, her eyes pooled with tears. 'You haven't heard, have you?'

'No, tell me…'

'Thomas and his friend went out for a run early this morning and…'

'Breathe, Nathalie. Take as long as you need,' Céline soothed.

'They went to the wood at the edge of the vineyard and they found him…'

'What do you mean? Who did they find?'

'Pierre… He had a noose around his neck… He was swinging from the branch of a tree,' she stammered. '*Il est mort.*'

Silence descended between them, heavy and sad.

'He was only twenty-four, he should be just starting out in life.'

'I'm so sorry…'

'It's a tragedy for his papa and for this community,' she said. 'We knew what was going on. We knew Pierre was struggling, and we just stood by and let it happen.'

'But what could you have done?'

Her expression turned from pain to anger. 'We should have stopped Luca. It is his fault.'

Céline gasped.

'He befriended Pierre and led him astray, introducing him to the dark world of drugs. Pierre clung to Luca, believing every word he said. But the drugs took control of him.'

Nathalie buried her head in her hands. 'What a tragic waste of a young life.'

Céline closed her eyes against the agony of what had happened. How she wished it was possible to turn back time, to change everything. 'My heart goes out to Gaston.' She bit her lip. 'He invited me for tea on Wednesday…'

'You must go, Gaston will need visitors,' she said, looking at Céline. 'So often when things like this happen, people avoid you, they cross the other side of the street. They don't know what to say…'

Céline nodded in agreement, silently vowing to visit him. 'How is Thomas?'

'He can't stop seeing the torment on Pierre's face and the glazed agony in his eyes.' She cradled her head in her hands, her body rocking back and forth. 'He will be plagued for a long time to come.' Her body heaved with sobs. 'Pierre died alone.'

'And what about Luca?'

Nathalie's face flashed with anger. 'We will *never* forgive him for this. Some of the workers have been to his house this morning and thrown rocks at his windows. There will be trouble, Céline, believe you me. He is responsible for this. He must pay.'

***

They sat in silence. Céline stared into the semi-darkness, trying to find the words to console the old gentleman consumed by his grief. Gaston had almost disappeared into the folds of his worn armchair, his body bent and twisted with pain. A vein on the centre of his forehead pulsated with agony, as he fixed his stare on the ground.

'Thank you for coming to see me, Céline, but I'm afraid I won't be very good company.'

She gave a wan smile. Even in his darkest hour, Gaston was worried about other people rather than himself. 'I can't imagine how you must be feeling right now, Gaston, but, if I can support you in any way, I'm here for you.'

His eyes drifted upwards. 'You're helping me just by being here. Why did he do it, Céline? *Pourquoi*? He is my boy, my own flesh and blood, and I love him.'

'It's hard to understand, but I like to think Pierre is at peace now.'

Gaston breathed shakily as he absorbed her words. 'I've never been a believer in God and the afterlife...' He let out a heavy sigh. 'I envy people who believe that there is a heaven up there, it must be very comforting. But how can we ever know?' He peered at her, searching for the answer to his question.

'I have always believed there must be something out there. We touch the earth briefly with our presence, but there must be more. Our earthly bodies die, but our soul lives on.' She paused to consider her words carefully. 'Pierre will always be with you, Gaston, in everything you do, and in all the memories you hold dear. It might not be a comfort to you now, but he will always be a part of you.'

'But he wasn't on the earth for long enough...'

Silence descended like a thick fog.

'I've been told that the workers are angry.' He shook his head sadly. 'I want everyone to remember Pierre with love, not with hatred and venom.'

'The community blames Luca for befriending Pierre and leading him astray.'

'I did too at the beginning. It was easier for me to lay blame at someone else's door – anyone – rather than think about Pierre. My poor boy had been struggling for many years, long before Luca came into his life.'

Céline listened quietly as Gaston poured out his grief.

'When he was a young boy, he was happy. Challenging at times, as all children can be, but he was cherished and loved by his mother and myself. But when his mother died…' He drew his fingers roughly through his hair. 'We were heartbroken. Life was never the same again. It was as if she was torn from us in the cruellest way. Pierre watched as his mother, the person he idolised, faded away in front of his young eyes. She was brave, Céline, but she could not hold in her pain towards the end. I still hear her chilling screams echoing in my head.' He covered his face with the palm of one hand. 'How could a nine-year-old ever recover from the loss of his mother?'

Céline offered him a sip of water to moisten his parched lips.

'We battled on, like two brothers against the world. I tried to compensate – to be both his father and his mother, but it wasn't enough. We loved each other very much, but I believe a mother's love for her child is irreplaceable.' His body heaved with pain. 'Pierre struggled as a teenager, friendless and alone. He was clever, loving and compassionate, but the teachers and the children at school didn't understand him. He was different, a misfit. He suffered from depression for most of his young life, and all I could do was to stand by and watch helplessly as he retreated into himself. I could do nothing, absolutely nothing to stop it.'

Céline listened to his sentiments, as the grandfather clock ticked relentlessly behind him. She could find no words that would comfort this broken figure sitting in front of her.

'I don't want Pierre to be remembered with anger and hatred. Luca extended the hand of friendship at a time when other people mocked Pierre or, worse still, treated him as an insignificant human being. Luca might have been a bad influence at times,' he said, shrugging his shoulders. 'But he was *not* the cause of Pierre's depression or of his untimely death.'

Céline looked in awe at this brave gentleman who, despite his grief, could eloquently articulate his thoughts: he expressed true compassion and generosity.

'I don't want Pierre to have died in vain. We must find it in our hearts to accept that Luca was not at fault, and to remember Pierre as a human being, special and unique, but damaged by circumstance...' He fixed eyes with Céline, determined in his resolve. 'I have not told you the full story. I have a few things I need to share, but, for now, I must rest.'

The next few days passed in greyness and misery. The community were mutinous in their belief that Luca was at fault and that he should be punished for the role he had played in Pierre's death. They whispered together, plotting how best to make Luca's life a misery. He had withdrawn into the shadows, and Céline was concerned for his safety.

One evening, as the community gathered around the fire pit, heads turned as Gaston slowly made his way into their midst, his body bent and his head bowed. Slowly, he lifted a shaky hand upwards to draw the attention of the crowd. A hush descended, the air heavy with anticipation, as everyone wondered what the wise old man would have to say.

Liz van Santen

Gaston gazed at the crowd in front of him, his tiny stature set with steely determination.

'This has to stop.'

The heavy weight of silence bore down around him.

'I loved Pierre. As a father, and as my closest companion. I am proud of what he achieved in his short life. He was sensitive and bright. He had so much love to give, but, since his mother died, he chose to take a lonesome path in life. He was consumed by grief, he adored his mother, and she was ripped away from our family in the most painful and torturous way. How can a nine-year-old boy process this?'

He breathed deeply, his face etched with pain.

'I tried to show my love for him. God knows, I tried.' He paused, drawing in breath through his clenched teeth. 'Nobody understood Pierre like I did… But there is something else. Something he chose not to share with me, or anyone else, for years.' He covered his face with his hands. 'If only he had confided in me. A parents' love for their child is unconditional.' He lifted his head and gazed into the wood smoke drifting up towards the night sky. 'I wouldn't have thought any less of him. It wouldn't have made any difference.'

Chapter 19

No one stirred as they listened to the words of a grief-stricken father and well-respected member of the community.

'We are all so quick to judge, we can be hard and unforgiving.' He paused. 'Perhaps this is how Pierre imagined I might think... One evening we sat together and he suddenly broke down in tears. I tried to comfort him, but he was inconsolable. I had never seen him as sad as this. But was it sadness? I saw terror in his eyes.'

Céline walked towards Gaston and put her arm around his shoulders. 'Perhaps you should leave this for another day?' she said, concerned for her new-found friend.

His jaw stiffened. 'No, I must carry on,' he said resolutely. 'That night my son "came out". He told me, through his sobs, that he preferred the company of men.' Gaston pulled himself up to his full height. 'You see, my son was gay. I can honestly say I felt nothing but relief. I had my suspicions for some time, and at last he was being open about his true feelings. I had imagined something truly terrible had happened to him... And I was right.'

The tension in the air was palpable.

'He suffered years of abuse and bullying at school, and I knew nothing about it.' Assaulted by wave after wave of emotion, the old gentleman looked unbearably fragile, like a leaf fluttering in the wind. 'He was sexually abused by one of the male teachers.' His body twisted with grief. 'My son was raped.'

Nobody moved or uttered a sound.

Gaston's shoulders shook with sobs that rose from deep within his belly. 'Pierre held all his strife and torment inside himself. He suffered in silence. I can't even begin to imagine his anguish… And I was powerless to help.' He curled the fingers of his right hand into a tight fist. 'But somebody helped him more than I ever could.' He scanned the faces of the people in front of him. 'It was Luca. He extended a hand of friendship, and became the brother that Pierre never had. Luca. He was not responsible for giving Pierre drugs. Those, I'm afraid, Pierre sourced himself.'

Everyone bowed their heads in shame, each reflecting on their own behaviour towards Pierre; their dismissive attitudes and judgmental views, and the harsh reality dawned that they must all share responsibility for Pierre's tragic death.

'We are all unique and special, regardless of our race, colour, disability, or sexual orientation. We must respect and love each other.' He paused, extending his tiny frame to full height. 'We are all different, and we need to celebrate differences. That's what makes the human race so special. I want good to come out of bad. I want Pierre to be remembered as a unique human being. Yes, damaged by life, but as a loving young man who had so much more to offer.'

A man in the front row started to clap his hands slowly, the sound ringing in the air. One by one, others started to join in, until the applause rose to a crescendo for the brave old man, his beloved son, and for the poignant words he had to say.

As the crowd dispersed, Gaston turned to Céline and acknowledged her with a weak smile. 'I hope they took heed of what I had to say.' His energy drained out of him, he limped slowly back towards his home, a broken but truly courageous man. Céline reflected on his words. She hoped that the workers were humbled by his sincerity and the important messages he shared.

The funeral was a sombre affair. Folk travelled far and wide to show their respect for a young man who took his own life. Gaston remained strong and dignified throughout, supported sensitively by individual members of the community. A lone figure stood to one side of the crowd that had now gathered around Pierre's unmarked grave. His shoulders shuddered, and tears of grief streamed in rivulets down his cheeks. Céline longed to comfort him, but she dared not. She turned away and when she looked again, Sophia was purposely striding towards Luca. She threw her arms around him and whispered something in his ear. He shot her a glance and roughly pushed Sophia away. With one last lingering look at the grave, he slunk into the darkness of the wood behind him.

A few days passed before Céline saw Luca again, and she noticed that he had changed since Pierre's death. It was as if the fire in his belly had been extinguished and had been replaced by something else, something Céline found hard to fathom. He had become more affectionate towards her, stroking her body softly and gazing lovingly into her eyes. She was puzzled by her own feelings, unsettled by his increasingly emotional advances. This had become more than a moment of physical pleasure; Luca was becoming emotionally involved with her and she knew this was not wise. She had to remind herself that she was a fugitive on the run from the authorities, she knew it was dangerous to get too close or emotionally attached to anyone. Sophia had become increasingly antagonistic and distant towards her, often angry and unpleasant. Céline was sure that she was fully aware about her meetings with Luca. Perhaps Sophia blamed her for Luca's public rejection of her at Pierre's funeral. She was also angry about the attention Pascal was giving her. Céline realised with regret that the time had almost come for her to leave the old house behind and move on to pastures new, before everything became too complicated.

***

27 March 1943

My body is exhausted and my mind in turmoil. I cannot rid my head of the death and destruction of this deadly war. The long dark nights are the worst. Agonising and vivid nightmares flash before my eyes and plague me to the depths of my soul. Will I ever forgive, or forget? I long to see my loved ones, my family, my friends, and my beloved

Beth, but I know I must bide my time, I must be patient. In the meantime, I pray with all my heart that they are safe and protected from the enemy.

But, just as the sun rises with the promise of a new day, I have a recurring dream. I am seven years old and I am running barefoot through the fields that surround our family house. I can feel the gentle wind brushing my cheeks and the soft earth, spongey beneath my feet. I am as free as a bird in flight. Life is full of anticipation and hope, I have joy in my heart. How I wish I could turn back the hands of time and experience the innocence and happiness of childhood one last time.

My work here in the vineyard is hard and relentless. Monsieur Renaurd, the owner, looks after the workers well. He asks no questions and provides comfortable accommodation, but in return, he expects hard work and high standards. The work in the fields is truly hard, but it distracts me from the horrors of my life, albeit for a fleeting moment in time. I'm surprised how much work there is to do in a vineyard during the winter months. The vines were pruned in February and now it is my job to check each vine meticulously, drive canes into the frosted earth, and attach the plants to each individual stake with thin wire, to support growth. I can't help but wonder where I will be when the vine flourishes and bears fruit. Will I survive to see another day, another month, another year? Or is my fate already sealed?

Stroking the cover of the journal gently with her index finger, Céline thought about the plight of Isaac Goldmann.

She felt privileged to be able to read an eloquent account of life during this period. She couldn't imagine the fear and torment that he, and millions of others, must have suffered during the hateful war. Lives destroyed, all hopes and dreams lost in an instant.

She knew she must finish the translation of the journal soon, so that she could share the content with Thomas. She wondered whether the driver of the lorry that transported Isaac Goldmann from Marseille to the relative safety of the vineyard could in fact have been Thomas's father. She relished the process of uncovering an individual story of life during this troubled time in history.

Staring dreamily out of the window, she considered the life and words of Isaac Goldmann that were emerging from the brittle pages of his journal. She would not presume to liken her life or her circumstances to that of Mr Goldmann: he was fleeing persecution, and almost certain death if he was discovered. Céline recognised that she did not have to endure the danger and perils of war expressed in his journal. But nonetheless, she felt an affinity with Isaac and his story. She too wished that she could turn back the hands of time and be a young child once again. Life then was full of excitement and questions. She was free to explore, discover and learn, without the inevitable weight of responsibility and worry that comes with the oncoming of adulthood.

She empathised with Isaac, and how he had to keep his Jewish religion, the very essence of his being, a secret from those around him, for fear of persecution. Céline, in her own life, understood what it felt like to be a fugitive, to be hiding her true identity, and to be harbouring a huge secret.

The vineyard had become a place of relative safety, a sanctuary, for both Isaac and herself. She imagined life in the vineyard during this period: the hard labour tending the vines, the agonising ache to be reunited with all those he held dear, the exhaustion and dread of being uncovered, and the overwhelming fear of death.

Yes, Céline felt a connection with Mr Isaac Goldmann. She could feel his spirit ever-present in the old house. All of a sudden, she felt a powerful surge of energy sweep through her body. Overwhelmed, she gasped for breath. At that moment she realised that she must take charge of her life. She must harness all her strength to forge a pathway into her future.

Her gaze turned to the chest of drawers where she had arranged a small posy of dried lavender, given to her by Luca during her last meeting with him. She absentmindedly brushed her hand gently over the tips of the faded purple flowers and inhaled the sweet aroma. She acknowledged that she was falling in love with Luca; his rugged earthy looks and his dark deep-set eyes were mesmerising, but there was more, a deep connection had grown between them where emotion – love, even – had transcended the necessity for words. A familiar fluttering bubbled up from deep within her and she lingered for a few seconds to grasp a rare feeling of true happiness.

Chapter 20

The following evening, Céline returned to the old house having enjoyed a long walk beyond the perimeter of the vineyard into the surrounding countryside. The fresh autumnal air had cleared her head and lifted her spirits, but now she was tired and she was looking forward to an early night. There was no one around, so she decided to devote some time to Isaac Goldmann's story before she fell asleep. As she opened the door to her bedroom, she froze. The wooden floor was strewn with lavender and the glass vase had shattered into tiny fragments. A feeling of nausea welled up inside her. She quickly scanned the rest of the room; everything else appeared to be just as she had left it.

The house was silent when she padded downstairs and into the kitchen. There she found Sophia sitting alone at the head of the table, her jet-black eyes glinting with fury. 'Well?'

'Well... what?' Céline stammered.

'You know exactly what I'm talking about. Who gave you the lavender?'

'I know this is your house, but what gave you the right to go into my room?' Céline suddenly remembered the time a few weeks before when someone had obviously rifled through her things. 'It isn't the first time, is it?'

'I'll ask again. Who gave you the lavender? Was it Luca? Was it my husband?' Her large birthmark disappeared within the deep furrows of her brow. 'Or perhaps you picked the posy for yourself,' she added sarcastically.

Céline looked away and bit her lip. She felt rather like a naughty child who had just been caught in the act of doing something wicked.

'Tell me,' Sophia shouted.

Céline locked eyes with Sophia. 'It was Luca,' she answered defiantly. 'He gave the lavender to me.'

'Well, that doesn't surprise me. I know all about your illicit meetings with him. I've followed you and I have witnessed with my own eyes what you have been up to.' The corner of her mouth twisted with rage.

'I could say the same about you, Sophia,' Céline muttered. 'Have you ever heard the phrase, "the pot calling the kettle black"?'

'Pot? Kettle? *Mon Dieu*, I have absolutely no idea what you're talking about.'

Céline tutted with frustration. 'I followed you to the outhouse on the night of the harvest party when you should have been by Pascal's side hosting the celebration. Instead, you were out enjoying selfish pleasure with Luca... I know where you go every evening.'

'So you admit it. You knew all along that Luca was mine, and you carried on regardless.'

'Luca is hardly yours, Sophia. You have a husband here at home. You can't monopolise someone like Luca.

He'll pick you up and drop you like a stone whenever it suits him. He's just a plaything for you, and we are just an amusing distraction for him... After all, life in the vineyard is probably rather monotonous.'

Sophia drew her fingers roughly through her hair.

'You must understand that in the beginning it was Luca who trapped me. He lured me into his arms and tantalised and pleasured me until I was at his mercy.' Céline hesitated. 'And then he forced himself on me. Some might call it sexual assault, or even rape. I didn't know what was happening... But I went along with it and, in the end, I allowed it to happen. Luca has a strange power over me, which I find hard to understand and impossible to resist.'

Sophia drew breath in surprise. 'That is exactly how Luca tempted me at the beginning. I had the same feelings, ecstasy, bewilderment, longing... And now I'm like putty in his hands.'

'Luca is not faithful to either of us, Sophia. He has many lovers in the community. He probably does exactly the same thing with all his conquests.'

Sophia nodded, the harsh reality slowly beginning to dawn on her.

'In my experience, men want everything,' Céline continued. 'They want a wife or long-term partner, and a variety of lovers as well. It's a herding instinct. I've seen it so many times before. Men are programmed to mate.'

'Maybe you're right...'

'Luca craves sex, just as I crave coffee in the morning when I wake up. He is just human, after all, he has desires and weaknesses, which he doesn't suppress. But there is a big difference between sex and love, Sophia. You can love someone from a distance.'

Sophia stroked her chin in thought. 'I think I'm beginning to understand what you're getting at,' she mused.

'And what of Pascal? Do you think he has needs and desires as well?'

'What do you mean? Pascal and I understand each other. We have an arrangement.'

'You have an arrangement that suits *you*, but does it suit Pascal?' Céline probed.

'We have a strong marriage, but you have turned his head. How could you? You come here, take advantage of our generosity, and you have ruined everything.' She threw her head in her hands. 'Everything.'

Céline pulled back a chair and sat down heavily, the length of the table separating the two women.

'You have attracted the two men in my life. Don't you understand? Without him, I am nothing.'

Céline stared at her in puzzlement. Was she referring to Pascal, or Luca?

'You are beautiful, Sophia, you draw attention wherever you go. You have a husband who adores you, he worships the ground you walk on. I do believe Pascal would sacrifice his own life to save yours.'

'So why does he want you?'

Céline considered her answer carefully. 'I think he's lonely. He sits here every night on his own, waiting for you to come home. One evening a few weeks ago, he was feeling particularly dismal, and so I invited him to share a bottle of wine with me…'

'Yes, I remember finding the wine stains on the table,' she said, absentmindedly drawing her fingers over its uneven surface. 'But it wasn't just a glass of wine, was it?'

She averted her eyes. 'Pascal is generous in giving you the freedom you have come to expect, but he has needs too. He longs for some affection.' She turned to look at Sophia. 'Do you show Pascal any love, something as simple as a warm hug or a kind word? Your relationship seems very one-sided to me: you have everything you want, and Pascal has nothing.'

Sophia lapsed into silence, immersed in her own thoughts.

'He is unique and precious, kind and compassionate; cling on to him for all you're worth. Consider your actions carefully, Sophia, or you might risk losing him for good.'

'I know,' she answered, 'but Pascal has never been enough for me. Luca makes me feel young and alive.'

'I find that, in life, we often don't appreciate what we've got until it's gone,' Céline said wistfully, reflecting on her own circumstances.

Sophia sighed heavily, her shoulders slumped. 'I'm not sure if I could survive without Pascal. I'm hot-headed, impetuous, I follow my heart rather than my head. Pascal is sensible, kind and thoughtful. He is my quiet voice of reason…' Her words faded away.

The two women sat in silence, each reflecting on their conversation.

'So, where do we go from here, Céline?'

'I think we have a lot in common. We have both been drawn in by Luca and his irresistible presence. Luca is a creature of the land. He is led by his natural instincts, and we have both succumbed.'

Sophia's voice softened. 'You are right. You, me and most women in the commune. Does this make us weak?'

'If he uses us to satisfy his own selfish desires then perhaps we are weak. But, on the other hand, if Luca makes us feel good, then what is the harm? You could even argue that we are using him. And, as far as Luca is concerned, you have no need to worry about me, Sophia. I will be leaving here soon, and I'm sure Luca will forget me in an instant.' As she said the last words, she didn't feel as if she was being entirely truthful; their relationship had already cut deeper than this.

'And Pascal?'

'I'm loath to give you advice, but if you want my humble opinion, I think honest and open communication is the key. Talk to him, Sophia. Tell him how you feel. How you really feel. Ask him how he is feeling. Is he happy? Listen carefully to him and respect his views. Sensitive conversations and affection between two people can solve so much in life.'

'I love Pascal, and I will talk with him. Thank you for your honesty, Céline. I have taken him for granted for far too long. You have given me a lot to think about.'

Céline moved her chair closer and cupped Sophia's hands in hers. 'Sometimes it takes an outsider to see these things. I feel sure it will make all the difference.'

'But I fear I'm addicted to Luca. I need him as much as I need food and water. How can I live without him?' Sophia bowed her head. 'I live with guilt every day...'

'Talk to Pascal, Sophia. You might find that, as you reflect on why you got together in the first place and rediscover the special love and connection you have between you, Luca might become less significant in your life. Until then, Pascal has given his blessing for you to see him. It will take time and patience, but you are strong, Sophia, and I feel sure that Pascal will wait until you are ready to let go.'

'I wish I had a fraction of your wisdom, Céline,' she mused. 'I wonder if we can reach an agreement? Of course, I am jealous that my husband is attracted to you – I can hardly blame him given the circumstances – but please will you stand back and give us the space and time we need to sort out our differences.'

'Of course, I have no wish to come between you and Pascal. I promise you.'

'And what I'm going to say next might surprise you. I think you should continue to see Luca until you leave us. If you are able to enjoy some brief moments of pleasure with him, then why not?'

Céline smiled. She must leave Sophia and Pascal to repair the cracks in their marriage without her interference, but Sophia had given her blessing for her to continue seeing Luca: to share him. The second part of the agreement seemed fairly unorthodox, but it would suit her well for the rest of her stay at the old house.

Sophia looked searchingly into Céline's eyes. 'Ever since I first met you, I've had the feeling that you are hiding a secret which has caused deep unhappiness and hurt in your life. I want you to know that If ever you feel the need to talk, then I am here for you.'

'Thank you,' Céline said softly.

The two women sat together, holding hands, basking in a warm and comforting glow of new-found friendship.

Chapter 21

'I have a proposition for you.'

Céline sipped her morning coffee and listened with interest to what Sophia had to say.

'My poor sister is struggling with her seventeen-year-old daughter, who has become belligerent and is now refusing to go to school. Monique used to be a bundle of fun, but now she is sullen and difficult,' she said, shaking her head sadly.

Cocking her head to one side, Céline wondered what all this had to do with her.

'She is a bright child, and my sister is worried about her education… but I'm afraid this is the least of her problems. Monique is being influenced by some of her friends – you know what it's like – smoking, drinking, drugs and all the other pressures that kids have to face these days. She's heading for disaster.'

'Oh dear, it can't be easy. Where do they live?'

'In the centre of Rouen, a large city quite a long way north from here.' She drew her fingers through her hair. 'I'm also really worried about my sister. She feels totally out of her depth with Monique, and I fear it's taking a toll on their marriage. So…' She looked directly at Céline. 'I've suggested to Sylvie that Monique comes to stay with us for a few weeks to give them a break. I wondered whether you would be prepared to give her some English tuition, on a casual basis, nothing too formal…'

Céline stared out of the kitchen window, taken by surprise at Sophia's suggestion. Her background was in teaching – she always enjoyed working with children – but she had never taught teenagers. She was worried that Monique would need more than she could offer. 'I'm not sure I'd be the right person to—'

'I have every faith in you, Céline,' she interjected. 'Whatever you do will be better than she is getting at home, and she'll escape all those bad influences. It will only be for a few weeks, and it seems like too good an opportunity to miss.'

'Would you want me to do this full-time, or are you talking about a short session every day?'

'I think two or three hours every morning would be enough. We can play it by ear.' She laughed. 'That's a funny English expression, isn't it?'

'It does sound like it might be good for Monique to come here for a while and have a complete change of scene,' Céline mused.

'It may kill two birds with one stone – oh that's another good English saying, isn't it – I'll pay you extra because I want to do my sister a favour. And, of course, you won't have to do as much housework. *Oui*? Please say you will.'

'You're sure it will only be for a few weeks?'

'Yes, about six weeks and then she will go back to her home in Rouen. Hopefully by then her parents will have sorted out their differences, Monique's behaviour will have improved... and, of course, she'll be top of the class in English,' she added with a grin.

'I'm willing to give it a go, but I can't promise to work miracles.'

Sophia's eyes sparkled with pleasure. '*Merci, ma chérie*, it's settled then. I'll ring Sylvie now to confirm arrangements,' she said, brushing Céline's cheek with her lips.

***

The car drew up in the midst of a cloud of dust. Sophia carried Monique's rucksack and suitcase to the front door, her shoulders hunched with exertion. 'Come on, for goodness' sake, Monique, take the suitcase, it's too heavy for me.'

She stood like a statue in the doorway, her eyes fixed on the floorboards in front of her. Her thick jet-black hair fell, covering one side of her face, the crown of her head encased within her raised shoulders, reminding Céline of a tortoise head ready to retreat into its shell. Her legs were long and gangly, the colour of mahogany, and barely covered by a grey strip of material that served as a skirt. A purple polo-necked sweatshirt skimmed over her well-formed figure, and a trendy pair of Converse trainers completed her look. But Céline's eyes were drawn to the index finger of her right hand, deeply stained with yellow, her nails dirty and bitten to the quick. Monique was a curious mix of effortless beauty of a young woman, and the stark awkwardness of a troubled child.

'Monique, I want you to meet my good friend, Céline.'

'I'm Moni, not Monique,' she mumbled through a mass of tangled hair.

'*Salut*, Moni, I've been looking forward to meeting you,' Céline ventured cheerfully. 'Did you have a good trip down?'

Sophia bristled past her and filled the kettle. '*Le Bouchon* the whole way. The traffic jams were endless. I don't know about you, but I'm gasping for a coffee. What a journey! It took hours.' She beckoned to Monique. 'Come and sit down, I'll show you up to your bedroom in a minute.' Sophia seemed to be intent on filling the empty void of silence with a constant stream of words. 'It's freezing out there, I think we're in for some stormy weather over the next few days.'

Monique remained silent, rooted to the spot.

'Just relax, Sophia, I'll make the coffee,' Céline offered.

'No, I need to move, my limbs ache from sitting still for too long. Moni, would you like a cup?'

Monique shook her head, her wide parting illuminated in the dim light of the kitchen. She mumbled something that neither woman could hear, and then she turned tail and sauntered out of the kitchen.

'*Merde*,' Sophia whispered under her breath. 'I think we're in for a very difficult few weeks.'

'We'll soon get her interested in something. She's just a moody teenager,' Céline said calmly, sensing that Sophia was tired, and her patience had already been tested to the limit. 'I'll show her to her bedroom.'

Monique slumped on the bed, staring dismally at the ground. Céline sat quietly beside her. The rain had started to fall and was now lashing the windowpanes with force. She glanced sideways to see Monique's shoulders heaving with anguish, her tears overflowing and running freely down her cheeks. 'No one listens…'

'I know what it's like to be far from home, and to feel lost and alone. I've been where you are now.'

'How can you possibly know?' she asked gruffly. 'No one understands how I feel.'

'Why don't you come down and join us for supper?' she said, putting her arm tentatively around Monique's shoulders. 'I've made some soup, and it's pretty good, even though I say so myself.'

Monique pulled back her shoulders, fiercely brushing the tears away from her face. 'I suppose I am quite hungry,' she conceded.

'And you could catch up with Pascal too.'

Supper passed smoothly enough, although the atmosphere was uncomfortable. Sophia was tired and crotchety, showing her annoyance by banging the soup terrine clumsily in the middle of the table, causing some of its contents to slop over the edge of the decorated bowl. Pascal ventured a few pleasantries about how lovely it was to see Monique, but his kind words fell on deaf ears. Monique slurped her soup noisily and said nothing. Céline glanced around, desperately trying to think of something – anything – to say. She excused herself and Monique as soon as she had cleared the table. 'It's been a long day. I don't know about you, but I'm up for an early night. How about you, Moni? *Bonne nuit*,' she added, as she and Monique turned towards the door.

After an unsettled night, Céline dragged herself out of the sanctuary of her bed, opened the shutters and cast her eyes across the vineyard. The storm had raged all night, but now there was a quiet lull and, although the low grey clouds raced across the sky, the rain had stopped, and there were promising patches of pale blue on the horizon. She thought wistfully about the morning routine she had enjoyed over the last few weeks, which always involved meeting Luca. This would no longer be possible, now that she would be working with Monique. She half wondered if Sophia had planned this deliberately, to thwart their meetings. She pursed her lips, resolving to find enough time in the day to give the young woman the time and attention she deserved, and to carve out time in the afternoon or early evening to see Luca.

Breakfast was a quiet affair. Monique toyed with her porridge, swirling it around in her bowl, but not eating very much. Pascal had left early to meet a supplier, and Sophia was busying herself clearing up the work surfaces and unnecessarily reorganising the cupboards.

'I think we should go for a walk this morning, as it's our first day together,' Céline suggested brightly. 'We can have a chat and perhaps practise a little English too.' She glanced out of the window. 'We can enjoy the fresh air at the same time.'

Monique lifted her gaze. '*D'accord*,' she agreed flatly.

Céline found Monique a spare pair of boots suitable for tramping the fields and, before long, they were on their way. As they left the old house in the distance behind them, Céline was the first to break the silence. She had already decided that today they would speak mainly in French to make it easier for Monique. 'Have you always lived in Rouen? I've never been there, but it sounds like a beautiful city.'

'Yeah, I've never lived anywhere else. I guess It's just like any other city,' she replied, 'dirty and big.'

'Isn't there a beautiful cathedral there?'

'Yes,' Monique replied quietly, 'I've only been there once... I liked it.' She hesitated. 'Did you know that Monet painted more than thirty views of the cathedral? I love his use of light and shadow...' Her words trailed away.

'Claude Monet? How interesting, I like his artwork too.'

'I went to an exhibition of his work last year,' Monique said, her voice less flat now. 'It was awesome. My favourite was his painting of a bridge over a lily pond.'

'Do you study art at school?'

'No, I had to take physics and chemistry instead. My parents insisted.' She stared resolutely at the ground. 'They want me to be a doctor or a lawyer.'

'And what do you think?'

'I want to be an artist.'

They followed the muddy path towards the end of the field. Céline quietly processed what this young woman had already shared with her. 'Do you draw and paint for your own pleasure?'

'Of course,' she said, her voice more animated now.

'I've brought my pad and pencils with me. I couldn't fit my acrylics into the rucksack.'

'Perhaps we could go into Marseillan and buy some paints for you to use while you're here.'

'Could we really?' she asked. 'My parents think I waste my time when I should be studying, but they don't understand. When I paint or draw, I'm in another world.'

Céline smiled. She was enjoying conversation with this bright articulate teenager. 'I would love to see some of your work. Have you brought anything with you?'

'I managed to squeeze my portfolio into my suitcase, but it meant that I had to leave my heavy physics and chemistry textbook behind.' She smiled. 'Do you really want to see my work? At home I hide my art under my bed. *Maman* occasionally shows interest, but *Papa* doesn't want to know.'

'I would really like to see it. I admire anyone who can draw or paint, I'm absolutely hopeless.'

'If you can hold a pencil, you can draw,' she said.

Chapter 22

15 April 1943

We had an unexpected visitor yesterday. The driver of the lorry – my guardian angel – who plucked me from imminent danger in Marseille, came to the vineyard to say hello. I was delighted to be able to thank him, and to find out a little more about him. His name is Thomas Debois. He travelled with his wife from Northern France to Marseille just before the beginning of the war. He passionately described his personal crusade to help the persecuted and oppressed to escape from the hands of the enemy. I felt honoured to meet Thomas and to be able to shake his hand. His bravery is quite extraordinary.

I dream about my darling Beth every day, I long to see her again and hold her in my arms. But I am ashamed to say that my head has been turned by Florence, a young woman who works in the kitchen. My body and my head are telling me different things. My body aches for her, but I know I must remain vigilant. I must not let down my guard. I must be faithful to my darling Beth. But I am sorely tempted by her buxom figure and her bright smile. I am confused and consumed by guilt.

Thomas Debois. Céline recalled her conversation with Thomas during their lunch at Marseillan a few weeks before. He told her that his father was a driver in this region during the war, and how he helped hundreds of marginalised people, persecuted by the Nazis: Jews, immigrants and underprivileged minorities. How he knew of trustworthy guides who would take them over the Pyrenees to Spain. *Papa was a good man with a heart of gold.* Could Thomas Debois be his father? She rubbed her hands together in excitement. She must visit Thomas and Nathalie as soon as she had finished the translation, and she would take the journal with her.

Her thoughts returned to Issac Goldmann, his love for Beth, and how his head had been turned by the temptations of the flesh. She could understand the shame and guilt he must have felt, but she also understood his longing for the simple comfort of being physically close to another human being.

***

Monique sat opposite Céline with a closed manila folder on the table in front of her. 'I must admit I feel a bit funny showing you my art, kind of exposed. I haven't shown many people…'

'I can understand that. It's your work, and it is personal to you. I would feel privileged to see what's inside, but only if you want to show me.'

She slowly opened the folder and spread her artwork across the table. Céline took a deep breath as she cast her eyes over a varied collection of drawings and paintings: rough sketches of the human form; life drawings and portraits; visual art depicting shocking discord within a city; the vibrancy of a busy high street set against a backdrop of poverty, homelessness and destitution.

Céline picked up every individual piece of art, handling each one as if it were a priceless possession.

'They could be better, couldn't they? I always have in my head what I want, but it doesn't always work,' Monique mumbled anxiously. 'Do you like them?'

Céline cast her eyes once again over the array of Monique's work. 'This collection is exquisite,' she answered. 'Truly remarkable.'

Relief flooded her face. 'I can't quite believe it. Nobody has really shown interest before. I have grown a thick skin, but I don't feel valued for what I think I do best.'

'I can understand that. I'm going to set a task for you to complete.'

'Is it going to be some horrible English translation, or learning boring verbs?'

Céline smiled. 'Actually, no. What I'd like you to do is make a few sketches. How does that sound?'

'Are you joking?'

'I'll explain. I would like you to make simple sketches of Sophia, Pascal and of me. In the next session, we will discuss your work both in French and in English. It will be good for your use of English and I hope it will be an enjoyable exercise. Oh, and bring your portfolio too.'

'Okay, that sounds great,' she said, her eyes shining with pleasure.

'And don't forget to ask Sophia and Pascal for their permission and explain why you are doing it.'

'Of course. Shall I make a rough sketch of you now?'

'As long as you show my best side...'

Monique selected a single piece of blank paper and paused, her pencil suspended in mid-air. She narrowed her eyes to appraise the model in front of her, making Céline feel rather uncomfortable.

'Just relax,' soothed Monique, 'it shouldn't take long.'

Céline watched out of the corner of her eye as Monique cut deliberate strokes across the paper, pausing only to examine the fine details of her face. She marvelled at Monique's power of concentration and her creative skills. She even looked different; radiant, more at peace with herself.

Monique paused again to stare for an unnervingly long time. She sucked the end of her pencil, deep in thought. Finally, she returned to her drawing and added an area of fine shadow to one side of the face. She studied her portrait, and then lifted her gaze. 'I have all I need to finish my drawing. Shall I bring it tomorrow morning for us to talk about?'

'That would be great. Don't forget to catch Sophia and Pascal, get their permission, and ask for a few minutes of their time.'

Monique carelessly shuffled her art collection back into her folder. 'It was better than I thought it would be,' she said. '*Merci bien, à tout à l'heure.*'

Céline was left alone with her thoughts. The session had not gone as she had planned; they had not spoken any English at all, but she was content with the outcome. Monique had shared her work and demonstrated her unique talent. She had a refreshing modesty about her own ability, or perhaps she was unaware of the extent of her considerable talent. It certainly seemed as if her parents were disinterested and unsupportive of her passion for art. Céline was convinced that this was the way that she was going to get to know and begin to understand the complex mind of this troubled teenager. She looked forward to their future conversations about the tasks she had been set. She couldn't help but wonder why Monique had lingered as long as she had whilst drawing her, and why she had added the area of shading on the left side of her face. She would remember to ask her tomorrow. But she was pleased with Monique's appraisal of their first session together: *It was better than I thought it would be.*

Later that day, Céline wandered along the path at the perimeter of the vines to the first of her early evening meetings with Luca. The light was beginning to fade, the sky laced with red, as the sun slowly fell over the distant fields. She was alone with her thoughts, feeling rather unsettled by the change in routine. She had noticed Sophia slipping out just before her session with Monique, and she was sure that she was on her way to see Luca. And now it was her turn. She pulled her coat around her as the wind caressed her cheeks. At last, she knocked on the door of the tall stone house. She was met by Luca, his hair brushed and tied back neatly. He wore a simple black T-shirt and faded pink shorts. He welcomed her into a large sitting room. The white walls danced with a rosy hue, reflecting the flames of the fire that burnt in a large open fireplace. A sheepskin covered the beige tiled floor in front of the fire, and a large basket stood to one side, full of logs gathered from the forest. Fairy lights cascaded over a green-leaved pot plant that leant over to catch the light from the shuttered window. A low terracotta sofa was positioned near enough to the fire to catch its warmth and comfort. '*Bonsoir, ma chérie*,' he said, kissing her gently. Céline caught her breath, she had rarely heard Luca speak in French; in fact, it was one of the first times she had ever heard him utter more than a few words.

'You speak French?'

'Of course,' he said, in a low gravelly voice, 'but I prefer the mother tongue. Would you like a glass of wine? Red, white or rosé?'

Céline felt strangely shy, this was not the Luca she had grown accustomed to, but she was beginning to enjoy herself. 'Rosé, please.' He beckoned her towards the large well-presented kitchen and pulled back one of two pine chairs for her to sit on.

'I can smell something delicious,' she said, extravagantly inhaling the mouth-watering aroma, coming from a cast-iron pan sitting on the hob.

'It's the season of *cèpes*,' he said, 'a special time of the year. I collected them myself from the woods this afternoon.'

'I have never heard of *cèpes*, Luca. What are they?'

'They are a mushroom, much sought after by anyone who loves food. I could never afford to buy them in the market, but I like to forage for my own.'

'Are they easy to find?'

'It is easy for me because I know where to look, but it's my secret. I will never tell anyone… not even you!' he added, with a smile. 'But, you have to be careful. There are many deadly mushrooms in the wood, it is easy to confuse them.'

Céline raised an eyebrow.

'Don't worry, I can recognise a *cèpe* from a death cap. Each year, foragers take their collection of mushrooms to the pharmacist to be checked, and last year, believe it or not, the pharmacist died of mushroom poisoning.'

Céline shivered and had to remind herself that Luca was a creature of the land; if anyone would know an edible mushroom from a deadly one, he would. She sipped her wine slowly, gazing at him as he cracked a few eggs into a bowl and whisked them into a pale froth.

'This evening, I'm making an *omelette aux cèpes*, one of my favourites.'

'*Ooh la la*,' Céline replied, sighing with pleasure. 'It sounds heavenly.'

He added a dash of milk and seasoning and poured the mixture over the simmering mushrooms. Taking a swig of his wine, he kept his eye on the pan until it was ready.

'*Voilà*,' he said proudly. '*Bon appetit.*'

As she tasted the first *cèpe*, the subtle creamy flavour delighted her taste buds. She beamed with pleasure. 'Luca, this is exquisite.'

The light of a candle in the middle of the table flickered, lighting up Luca's face as she watched him devour his food with pleasure. '*Cèpes*, like the fruit on the vine, are a priceless bounty of the land.'

'"Priceless bounty of the land",' she said, echoing his words. 'What a beautiful way of describing the richness of the earth. I like to eat local produce – fruit and vegetables – in season, they taste fresh and special. It seems a shame to freeze blackberries that you have picked in the autumn, to eat – less full of flavour – in the spring.'

Luca lifted his gaze and nodded in agreement. 'We have a special connection, you and I, Céline, something happens when we are together.' He paused. 'I'm not just talking about sex…' He paused again. 'Although sex with me is exciting, I know how to please a woman.' He looked tenderly at her. 'I long to touch your body, but I also want to connect with your mind.'

Céline put down her knife and fork. 'What about all the other women in the commune that you have seduced?'

'They mean nothing to me. It is harmless. I satisfy my needs, and they enjoy it too. It's a break from a very hard life. What is wrong with a little pleasure? It is just normal, *n'est pas*?'

'But do you think it is right?'

He stared into the distance. 'It is all I have ever known… I don't think I've ever caused harm. It's never been my intention.'

Céline sighed. She struggled with his attitude and his way of life, but how could she possibly criticise him? 'And where does Sophia fit into this?'

'She craves my attention.' He bowed his head. 'I feel bad when I'm with her. I've wanted to stop seeing her for months now, but she keeps coming back for more. What can I do?' He threw his arms in the air. '*Merde*. She gave me this place. I'm in her debt, and she knows it.'

'Do you ever think about Pascal?'

'Yes, I do. I like Pascal very much, and I don't think he's happy. But he goes along with it for Sophia.'

'So you are hurting someone.'

'I suppose I am,' he mused. His deep brown eyes bored into hers. 'But you, Céline, you are different.'

Chapter 23

She spread three drawings across the table. '*Voilà*, I've done as you've asked.' Monique gave a bashful smile. 'They're just sketches, I didn't spend long on them. But I guess they're not too bad,' she said, shrugging her shoulders.

Céline studied each drawing in detail before looking up. It was remarkable how Monique had, with just a few strokes of the lead, been able to capture both the physical and characterful features of each face. Sophia: beautiful, sexy, impetuous... Pascal: pale-skinned, with misty blue eyes showing sadness, heartache, anguish, but also shining with kindness, generosity and sensitivity. It was as much about the marks that the artist had not made on the page, as those that she had. Monique had captured the very essence of Sophia and Pascal.

Monique sat still, biting the nails of her right hand. 'Are they okay? Are they what you wanted me to do?'

Céline smiled at the anxious young woman sitting in front of her. 'They are expressive and beautiful.' She cast her eyes over each sketch again. 'Now, I'd like you to tell me the story that you had in your mind when you were studying each face. In French first of all, and then we will try some English.'

Monique's features softened with relief. 'Well, Sophia was quite hard to pin down. She never sits still, so it was a bit like trying to capture a still image on a moving target... Like painting a countryside scene from a speeding train. But when she was reading a message in her notebook, I grabbed a fleeting moment.' She gave a wry smile. 'I think she must have been reading something raunchy because she had a wicked expression on her face.' She hesitated. 'I don't mean *wicked* as in like a bad person. I mean *wicked* as in holding a guilty, pleasurable, secret.'

'How interesting, Moni,' she replied, her thoughts racing. 'You've made me wonder who the message was from, and what it was about.'

'We might never know. And *not knowing* is a great place to be – a mystery – it makes my creative juices flow. Sophia is flamboyant and carefree on the outside, but I think there is something, or someone, lingering just beneath the surface. There is a lot more to Sophia than meets the eye.'

Céline pondered her words, marvelling at Monique's extraordinary insight, and her ability to look beyond the obvious.

'And Pascal,' Céline said, selecting the next piece of sketch. 'What were your thoughts while you were studying him?'

'Pascal is complex and strong. He doesn't allow his albino features to define who he is; in fact, he plays it to his advantage, and it adds to his whole persona. His love for Sophia is almost palpable, and I hope I've captured this in my drawing.' Her brow creased with emotion. 'But there was something else, something deeply troubling, about him. He is kind, thoughtful and hard-working, but his heart is breaking.'

Céline listened in wonderment. How a teenager, only seventeen years on this earth, could possibly have such a rare talent for art, and also have the ability to uncover hidden depths of her subjects, was quite beyond her; it was rather like listening to the views of a clairvoyant. There was something unsettling about hearing what Monique had to say about her next drawing.

'Well, last but not least,' she said, trying to make light of the next conversation. 'What did you find out about me?'

'I see a beautiful face, kind, gentle and empathetic. I'm puzzled by the colour of your hair. It's black, but you have blonde features. Most of my friends would kill to be blonde...'

Silence descended between them.

'It's funny, I've always wanted black hair, I think it's more striking,' Céline answered, rather unconvincingly.

'Really? I like blonde hair.' Monique returned her gaze to the drawing in front of her. 'You have an open face, full of curiosity. I think you have a thirst for learning, and a passion for teaching. For you, it is all about sharing knowledge and experience and connecting with people.'

'So why have you covered part of my face with shading, Moni?' she asked, not entirely sure that she wanted to hear the answer.

'I think you are concealing something terrible that has happened in your life. You are running away rather than facing your demons. I can see it in your face.' She stared deeply into Céline's eyes. 'You hide behind a mask.'

Céline averted her gaze, unnerved by Monique's comments. She couldn't believe that her eyes could give so much away; that she was this transparent.

'I'm in the glorious place of unknowingness again,' said Monique. 'I hope you're okay with my drawing and my thoughts?' She paused, waiting for a response, but Céline remained pensive, silent. 'I haven't spoken a word of English yet. Would you like me to talk you through my drawings again, this time using my useless English?'

Céline swallowed a large gulp of air, realising that she had held her breath for far too long. 'Yes, but before you do, I need to congratulate you, both on your incredible sketches and on your analysis of what you can see beyond the physical. You are amazing.'

Moni beamed. 'Now I try in English, but I zink many times I get it wrong.'

***

Céline felt unsettled after her morning session with Monique. She worried that her past was catching up with her rather faster than she had hoped. Moni was not only a talented artist, but she was a young person who could look beyond the surface, beyond the skin and bones, and burrow deep into the heart and soul. And Céline had been too taken aback to deny anything. She began to wonder if Sophia and Pascal were beginning to suspect anything. She must not let her mask slip. Lifting the rug, she prised open the floorboard and reached for the journal, thinking that the words of Isaac Goldmann might offer some distraction.

3 May 1943

I have made a deadly mistake, one that I fear might cost me my life. I let down my guard and succumbed to the pleasures of the flesh with Florence, the young woman who works in the kitchen. How could I have been this weak? This stupid? I wooed her into my bed, and I bore myself to her. Her eyes were immediately drawn to a feature of my body that defines me for who I am. A Jewish man. I saw an expression of shock and disbelief flash across her face. I don't trust her. I suspect she intends to betray me and inform the authorities of my whereabouts. There is no time to waste. With God's speed, I must leave tonight.

Céline digested the words on the page, her heart beating against her ribcage. Her hands shook as she turned over the brittle page. It was blank. She turned over the next page. It was blank. There were no more entries in Isaac Goldmann's journal. Her eyes misted with tears. She had so many questions spinning around in her head. Did Florence betray him? Where did he flee to that night? Did he escape? Was he captured by the enemy? She stared forlornly at the faded page. Perhaps she would never know Isaac Goldmann's fate. He had become a special feature of her life. Although she had never met Isaac, and knew little about him, she had grown to love his writing and the sometimes heartwarming, sometimes harrowing, account of his daily routine. She felt honoured to have been able to read an account of a short but significant part of his life.

But now it had come to an abrupt end, like a train hitting the buffers. She felt bereft, overcome by an enormous sense of loss.

She opened her computer and checked that she had made an accurate record of every entry of the journal, dating from 3 September 1937 to 3 May 1943, both in the original text, and the English translation. After saving each document in a single named folder – "A Fellow Fugitive" – she turned off the computer and carefully closed the lid.

She checked the time. Yes, she would have enough time to visit Thomas. She felt a strange urgency to talk to them about Isaac Goldmann and what she had discovered. And what she hadn't.

As she knocked on their door, she clutched her bag close to her, suddenly sensing the end, like she often felt after she had finished a great novel, but more so. Thomas opened the door and welcomed her in. She had noticed that he had lost some of the light in his eyes since the day he had discovered Pierre hanging from a tree. It still haunted him.

'Thomas, it's really good to see you.'

Engulfing her in his arms, he looked down at her with concern. 'Are you okay, *ma belle*?'

She lingered for a few seconds, enjoying his warmth and comfort. 'I have something I want to share with you. Is Nathalie around?'

'No, she's taken the kids for a walk.' He sighed. '*Merde,*

they need to let off steam, they've been impossible today. Anyway, come and sit down, and tell me all.'

She sat heavily in the soft armchair. 'Do you remember I told you about a journal that I found under the floorboards in my bedroom in the old house?'

Thomas nodded, raising his eyebrows with interest.

'Well, I've finished reading and translating the text, and now I want to hand it over to you. Thomas, the ending was a shock. One day Isaac wrote a diary entry, and then... Nothing. It has left me feeling rather lost, bereft. I need to know what happened to him...' She wrung her hands together. 'Did he manage to escape, or was he captured? Did he live to see out the war or...'

'I think we need a Pastis, and then I want you to tell me more,' he suggested.

As she sipped the cool aniseed drink, Céline wondered where to begin. 'I've already told you about how Isaac Goldmann, a Jewish gentleman, escaped from the round-up of the Jews in Marseille in 1942.'

'Yes, I remember...'

'Isaac was given a lift by the driver, who he called his guardian angel, and he was taken by night to the vineyard. When I told you that part of the story, Isaac didn't know his name.'

'And?' he asked eagerly.

Céline swallowed, willing the driver to be Thomas's father. 'Later on, the driver returned to the vineyard, and Isaac was able to thank him. His name was Thomas Debois.'

Thomas stared at her, open-mouthed, his body braced with tension and anticipation. 'No,' he said, 'Thomas was not my father.' He glanced upwards and gazed into her eyes. 'But he was my father's best friend. They worked together during the war to rescue the persecuted. Thomas was a truly courageous man, and together with my father, Samuel, they saved many lives. I am proud to have been named after him.' He lifted his shoulders and smiled wistfully. 'But no, Thomas was not my father.'

Céline waited quietly, absorbing what he had said. 'Do you know what happened?' she asked quietly.

'*Papa* and Thomas survived the war, but I don't know what happened to Isaac Goldmann.' He hesitated. 'It's strange that he left the vineyard, but he didn't take his journal with him. He must have left in a hurry for whatever reason. The old house might have been raided, he might have been captured.'

They sat in silence, each wrapped up in their own thoughts.

'Isaac knew he'd made a terrible mistake that might cost him his life. He had sex with a kitchen hand, and it was then that she discovered that he was a Jew. In his final diary entry, he suspected that she might inform the authorities. I think this is exactly what happened. Florence betrayed him.'

Thomas folded his arms. 'Now that we have this journal, we might be able to find out more about what actually happened. It might be that Isaac managed to escape over the Pyrenees and to safety.'

Céline didn't want to consider the alternative.

Reading her thoughts, Thomas continued. 'He was obviously a brave and wise man, let's wait and find out more before we pre-empt his fate.' He sipped his Pastis. 'I'm very much looking forward to reading the journal, Céline. This is significant, a *real* account of *real* people during this time. It is very different from the dusty textbooks of my history class when I was at school. I'm sure this will bring to life all the feelings and emotions, as well as the events during this period of the war.' His eyes shone. 'What a find.'

Chapter 24

'I need to speak to you urgently,' Sophia hissed. 'Come to the courtyard now.'

Céline looked at her in surprise. What could possibly be this urgent? 'Okay, I'll just finish the drying up and I'll be there.'

'No. Now.'

Drying her hands with a damp tea towel, Céline hurried out of the kitchen towards the courtyard, feeling nervous about what Sophia could possibly have to say that was so urgent.

'I've got symptoms.'

Céline looked at her, her brow furrowed in puzzlement. 'Of what, Sophia?'

'I've got a strange feeling down there,' she whispered, pointing to her crotch. 'I'm itchy and it stings when I...' She shook her head. 'I think I must have caught something.'

The truth began to dawn. 'You think you might have an STI?'

'STI?'

'A sexually transmitted infection.'

Sophia hit her forehead with the flat of her hand. 'It must be Luca. I can't have caught it from anyone else.'

'*Putain*,' Céline muttered. 'I could have it too. And most of the women in the commune, and their husbands. Pascal?'

'No, Pascal should be okay... Shouldn't he?' Sophia added accusingly.

'I think everyone should be tested,' Céline said firmly. 'Have you told Luca?'

'No, not yet.' A single tear escaped the corner of her eye. 'But I will have to, won't I?'

'I think the first thing we should do is to get tested, don't you think? It might not be an STI, it might be as simple as a dose of thrush or cystitis. You might just need a course of antibiotics,' Céline said, gently holding one of Sophia's clammy hands. 'It's probably nothing, but better to be safe than sorry.'

'Perhaps we both should have thought about this before we had unprotected sex with Luca,' Sophia muttered.

Céline pursed her lips. She hadn't given it a second thought. She had always suspected that she was infertile, so there was never a risk of an unwanted pregnancy, but she really should have been aware of the importance of safe sex. She should have known better.

After lunch, the two women made their way by car to Marseillan to the sexual health clinic. The atmosphere on the journey was sombre, compounded by dark heavy clouds that littered the sky, and a group of moustached men wearing bright-orange gilets, spaced out along one side of the road, facing the forest. They looked menacing as they hugged their guns close to their chests. Watching and waiting.

'What are they hoping to shoot? They seem dangerously close to the road for my liking.'

'Anything they see: wild boar, pheasants, deer... This is how the French organise the shoot, and it's the beginning of the shooting season.'

'And what about those people over there?' Céline asked, pointing to a small group of people, foraging underneath a clump of oak trees. 'I hope they don't get shot by a stray bullet. They're holding wicker baskets, what are they searching for?'

'They're out looking for *cèpes*, a special kind of mushroom. You can find them around the trunks of *le chêne* – the oak tree – at this time of the year. You need a keen eye, the mushrooms are well camouflaged and difficult to spot amongst the undergrowth.'

Céline's thoughts returned to the delicious *omelette aux cèpes* that Luca had prepared for her less than a week ago. But things were different now: the thought of a sexually transmitted disease cast a stain on everything. She had enjoyed their spontaneous reckless sex together, but now everything was spoiled.

'Are you more worried about being tested, or finding out the results?'

'If it's bad news, the thing that worries me the most is the impact this will have on the commune, and on Luca. I'm sure he had no idea that he could be spreading disease.' Céline let out a deep sigh. 'How on earth can all his sexual partners be contacted, named and treated?'

'That is something for Luca and the medical services to deal with and I will let him know straight away. Luca must take responsibility for his actions.' Sophia gripped the steering wheel with force. 'We have all been very naïve.'

'But Luca is a wild creature, I wonder if he is even aware about the dangers of promiscuity.'

'Well, if he wasn't aware before, he sure as hell will be now.'

They rang the bell and entered the waiting room. A row of metal chairs were arranged on the cold lino floor. The institutional green walls were bare, except for a large sign informing patients that staff expected to be treated with respect, and any abuse would not be tolerated. A stern bespectacled woman in her late fifties, wasting no time with pleasantries, recorded their details on the clinic's database. Céline breathed in the smell of disinfectant, mildly disguised by the pungent scent of a large, slightly withered, vase of lilies perching precariously on the corner of her desk.

After an endless wait and a raft of tests taken by an unsympathetic clinician, they left, their heads bowed in remorse and shame, each clutching a handful of pink-and-blue leaflets informing them about the importance of sexual health.

The journey home was gloomy and quiet. A dark thought crossed Céline's mind. Could she have caught the infection in Marseille and passed it on? Surely not. She had no symptoms.

The two women would have to wait a week to confirm the results. But they already knew.

***

Monique clutched her portfolio nervously, the yellow nicotine stain clearly visible on the index finger of her right hand.

'What is it, Moni? You don't look happy today.'

'It's just… I suppose I'm worried about showing you my sketch.'

'I'm not here to judge, it will be a good starting point for discussion. And useful for practising your English too.'

Monique reluctantly pulled out a single piece of drawing paper and placed it between them, facing Céline so that she could study it from the other side of the table. She quietly absorbed the subject of the drawing. The paper was divided into two by a thick jagged line. On one side of the divide, Monique had drawn her parents in physical confrontation. Her father towering over her mother, his arm outstretched, the palm of his hand extraordinarily large, poised to bare down on one side of her face. Her mother's features distorted; body bent, rigid, braced for the inevitable.

An image of Monique occupied the other side of the sharp divide; slumped against the wall, her knees tightly drawn to her chest, her face concealed by a clump of tangled hair, and hands tightly clamped over her ears. She was surrounded by pieces of artwork, some screwed up, others ripped in half. Beside her stood a half-consumed bottle of vodka and an empty packet of *Gauloise*, a French brand of strong cigarettes.

The drawing depicted the unspeakable horror of parents at war, and the utter hopelessness and vulnerability of a young woman, a daughter: the juxtaposition of anger and despair.

'You see, it doesn't matter who I am, all that matters is who *they* want me to be.'

Céline looked benevolently at the crushed teenager in front of her, absorbing the shocking and graphic portrayal of her life, and the poignancy of her words. She had tasked Monique with making a sketch of her parents and herself in their house in Rouen, and the detail on the page told her everything. The damage that parents can cause – perhaps inadvertently – is extraordinary and significant. Monique's parents wanted her to be a lawyer or a doctor, believing this to be the best option for a secure future, but they have closed minds to any aspirations or dreams their daughter might have. Her parents have not listened. Something must be done, before it is too late.

'Moni, do you feel safe at home?' Céline asked quietly.

'Yes I do,' she mumbled. 'The fighting doesn't happen often, but when it does, I hide in my room or I go and meet my friends. They always argue about me.' Her shoulders shook with emotion. 'It is all my fault.'

'None of this is your fault, Moni. Does your father hit you?' Céline asked, reaching over to gently stroke one side of her face.

'No, he doesn't, but he scares me sometimes.' Her eyes widened with fear. 'And I worry about *Maman*. I always think I should be at home, just in case...'

'Would you mind if I talked to Sophia about this?'

Moni silently nodded in agreement.

'It might all seem overwhelming and insurmountable at the moment, but it will get better. Talking through problems can really help. And we are all here to listen. The only thing I would say is that alcohol won't provide any answers.'

'Maybe not, but it numbs the pain.'

Céline looked at the misery and the burden of responsibility etched in her young face and sensed that this was not the time to pursue this painful conversation. She must talk to Sophia. 'Let's leave this for now, but we can talk again soon. I think you are brave, thank you for sharing such a personal part of your life. And remember, we are here for you.'

Céline was the first to break the silence. 'I'm intrigued, Moni, what's in your bag? Did you bring something to show me?'

'Oh I nearly forgot, I brought a present for you,' she said, pulling out a round parcel wrapped loosely in a bundle of newspaper. 'It reminded me of you, so I thought you might like it.' She placed the heavy object on the table and carefully unwrapped the newspaper to reveal a large snow globe. Céline clutched it in her open palms and shook the glass ball. In the midst of a thick snowstorm stood the straight-backed figure of a lone woman clad in a thick winter coat, one booted leg striding forward towards the mountains that dominated the dark skyline. Her jaw dropped in surprise. 'This is beautiful.'

'I like it too. There are so many snow globes with chocolate box views of chalets, snowmen, Santa in his sleigh, and sparkly pine trees, but this is far more interesting. I like to imagine where the woman is going, and I wonder why she is alone.'

'The style of her coat was popular during the nineteen-forties, perhaps it is wartime,' Céline mused.

'There is something about the way she is striding towards the mountains, she seems fearless and brave. I like to think of her as a strong independent woman, confronting the eye of the storm without turning back.' She paused. 'She will get through the darkness, and find the light, I just know it.'

'Why does she remind you of me?' Céline asked, dubiously.

'Because you have been through dark times in your life. You will face your demons – it might take time – but you, just like the lone woman in the globe, will find peace in the end. I promise you, I see it in your eyes.'

'She reminds me of you too, Moni. You are in a stormy time right now, but you are strong and talented, you will find a pathway through.'

Céline sighed heavily. 'Good grief, this is all a bit deep and meaningful isn't it?' They both laughed. 'But thank you, Moni, I will treasure this gift and it will always make me think of you,' Céline offered, idly smoothing out the layers of newspaper on the table.

Suddenly, the colour drained from her face. She stared at the words in front of her.

'What's the matter?' Monique asked, following the line of Céline's vision to a photo of a woman, positioned above the following notice:

MISSING PERSON:
Wanted in connection with an unexplained death in Oxford.
Libby Wilkinson
Age: 42
Height: 5′4
Hair colour: Blonde
Last seen: Salcombe. Believed to have formerly resided in Oxford.
If you know where Libby is, or have any information regarding her whereabouts, please call Oxford or Salcombe police:
01865 435896 (Oxford) or 01548 353824 (Salcombe)
Can you help? Reward offered.

Monique narrowed her eyes to study the features of the woman in question. 'She looks just like you.'

Céline stared down at the notice, her hands damp and clammy.

'She has the same eyes, and a freckle on the side of her face.' She turned abruptly to face Céline. 'It *is* you.'

Chapter 25

'Have you ever heard of the word "doppelgänger"?' Céline asked, thinking on her feet. 'It's when people have strikingly similar features. Sometimes they can even be mistaken for twins.'

'Yes, I do remember reading an article about this. I suppose it is possible, but I study faces,' she said. 'Where did you live in England?'

'All over the place, mainly in the south. I was rather a nomad.'

'It's your business, not mine. But I do prefer your hair blonde.'

Silence descended between them.

'Don't worry, I won't tell anyone.'

'I'm surprised you have English newspapers, this is *The Sunday Times* from a few weeks ago,' Céline said, her voice wavering.

'My parents think that if I read English papers, I will suddenly become a master of the English language,' she said, clicking her fingers in the air. 'But I prefer *Paris Match*.'

'Thank you for my wonderful gift, Moni, I will treasure it.' She hurriedly bundled the globe in the newspaper and put it to one side of the table. 'Now, where were we?'

The rest of the session was uneventful, each distracted by their own thoughts.

After lunch, Céline retired to her room. She had a lot to think about. She carefully unwrapped the snow globe and placed it on her chest of drawers, but it was the newspaper article that she was more interested in. She knew that Moni had been unconvinced by her feeble attempt to provide an explanation. She spread each page of *The Sunday Times* across her bed, smoothing away the creases with the flat of her hand. She took some comfort in the fact that the article was buried deep in the middle pages of the paper, but the photo was a clear likeness and, although she felt reasonably safe here, Monique knew, and it wouldn't take long for word to spread.

She scanned the rest of the newspaper until she came to page eight: *Book Reviews.* The words hit her like a punch in the gut.

The Humble Pawn
Author: Antonia Farouk
Number One Sunday Times Bestseller
Brilliant, a page turner, a must-read, edgy, unique…
*Note: The author, Libby Wilkinson, chose to write under the pseudonym, Antonia Farouk, and is now listed as a missing person.

For a fleeting moment, her heart swelled with pride. Her story – *The Humble Pawn* – was an acclaimed bestseller. If she had been leading a "normal" life, she would now be famous; she would be recognised as a respected author, and she would, without doubt, be quite wealthy. Céline could hardly believe the words on the page. She didn't consider herself to be an exceptional writer, or even a good one, but here it was in black and white, for everyone to see.

She read the article over and over again. Buried deep within hundreds of comments, one reviewer had written: "An intriguing read, made even more mysterious by the sudden inexplicable disappearance of the author, now wanted in connection with an unexplained death. Readers of this book will all be asking the same question – Is *The Humble Pawn* fact or fiction?"

Back in England, she was famous, as an author and as a missing person, wanted by the police. She will be the subject of much debate. Questions will be asked. How did she disappear? Where is she? Did she commit murder? Did she take her own life?

Is *The Humble Pawn* an autobiography?

Her attention turned to the snow globe, the lone woman, facing the eye of the storm. Shivers ran up and down her spine. She knew what she had to do.

***

'*Bonjour, Thomas*. Thanks for agreeing to see me at such short notice.'

'Come on, Céline, we haven't known you for very long, but you don't need an appointment to see us,' he said, laughing.

Céline dug into her bag and pulled out a snow globe, portraying a man and a woman walking through the snow. 'I almost forgot to give you this. It was under the floorboards with Isaac Goldmann's journal. I think you should have it.'

'*Ooh la la*, another piece of history in the making… I wonder if Isaac imagined he was walking with his beloved Beth through the snow?' he said, gently fondling the curved surface of the globe. 'I would like to think so.' His eyes lit up. 'I have nearly finished reading the journal. Luckily my German is good enough to understand it. What a fascinating account. I intend to take it to the local museum and discuss with them where the journal should be displayed, perhaps in a museum close to the town of his birth. It has been such a privilege to read Isaac's diary, thank you for sharing it with me. We should probably mention this to Sophia and Pascal, as you found it in their house, I'm sure they'll feel the same as me.'

Thomas paused, gazing at her with concern. 'You look upset. Talk to me. What on earth is going on?'

'Brace yourself, Thomas. What I am about to tell you will come as a shock.'

Her words came tumbling out.

'I don't know where to begin,' she whispered. 'I'm not who you think I am. My name is not Céline Dupont, I've been living a lie.' She bowed her head. 'My name is Libby Wilkinson.'

'But why? I don't understand.'

'Two years ago, I was living and working in Oxford, and I was married to…' Her face crumpled with pain. 'Alex. He was a well-respected lawyer in an Oxford firm of solicitors.'

'*Mon Dieu*, it didn't occur to me that you might be married.'

'At first, everything was exciting and new, we had the world at our feet. We loved each other…'

'So what happened?'

'We wanted to start a family. We tried, but it seemed that I couldn't give him the very thing he wanted. We had a lot of tests, but the fertility clinic couldn't find any reason why we couldn't conceive, they called it "unexplained infertility". But I think it was all my fault,' she muttered. 'I suffered from anorexia nervosa when I was a teenager, and I must have done irreparable damage.' She looked up, her eyes pooled with tears. 'He called me *the womanless woman*.'

'How could he?' Thomas asked, throwing his arms into the air in disgust. 'You are a beautiful woman, Céline, any man would be proud to be with you.'

'After that, Alex began to undermine me, putting me down. He even took away my car keys… I believed his cruel words. I felt worthless.'

'*Merde.*'

'He made me doubt myself. The guilt, the shame… You don't want to hear all this, but it helps me to explain what happened.'

Thomas leant forward, listening intently to what she had to say.

'At times he could be so kind and attentive. When he was like that, I could almost believe that he didn't mean the unkind words, that he actually loved me…' She paused. 'But then he would change like flicking a switch.'

She wrung her hands together. 'But despite everything, I loved him.'

Thomas cupped her hands in his. 'Céline, it sounds like he emotionally abused you. He controlled and manipulated you. If I ever met him, I would give him a piece of my mind,' he muttered angrily.

'I can see this now, but at the time I was confused and vulnerable. He betrayed me. He cheated on me with another woman. I suspected it, but I kept pushing it to the back of my mind.'

'How the hell could someone as lovely, kind and intelligent as you, end up with that sorry excuse for a man?'

Céline stared into the distance, oblivious to his remarks.

'We went to Paris for a weekend with another couple, Roland and his wife.' She paused. 'It's hard to believe, but Roly's wife was the woman Alex was having the affair with.'

'*Ooh la la*! Did you have a big fight?'

'They had an open marriage, so it was okay for them,' she said, shrugging her shoulders. 'We went to Chez Fleurie, a libertine club, just outside Paris.' Céline bit her lip, suddenly nervous that he would be shocked by her revelation.

'Really? Chez Fleurie is a prestigious club, one of the best of its kind in Europe. Did you enjoy it?'

'I felt rather out of my depth initially, but I have no regrets. I learnt a lot about myself, and about Alex. When we were in the dungeons,' she glanced at Thomas, 'I was surprised to find that he chose to be submissive – to be tied up, restrained. I was used to his dominant, controlling behaviour, so it shocked me; it seemed so out of character. But it appeared to make him happy. Watching him restrained with a collar and chain gave me an idea for a birthday treat.'

'*Vraiment*?'

'I know it sounds strange, but I just wanted to do something that he might enjoy. I desperately wanted to save our marriage. But it was one of the biggest mistakes of my life.' She buried her head in her hands. 'If only I could turn back the clock…'

Thomas listened as the story emerged.

'Anyway, when we got home, his illegitimate son, Tai, appeared on the doorstep. Alex had no idea he had a child. It's a long story, but it was then that I found out the true horror of his conception. Alex blurted out the truth. I can't find the words, Thomas, it's just too awful.'

A thick and heavy silence filled the room.

'But it explained everything: Alex's dismissive attitude towards women, and his cruel and controlling behaviour. This discovery made me even more determined to save our marriage, so I went ahead and organised the birthday treat. I knew that he enjoyed being submissive so I asked two friends to help me choreograph an exotic dance, performing in front of Alex, who was chained to the bed. I really thought he would love it… And he did. But then something terrible happened.' Her body shook with emotion.

'After the dance, we left Alex tied up, because that is

what I thought he enjoyed, and we went to have a drink. When I returned I…'

'Take your time…'

'He wasn't breathing. It looked as if he had choked on his own vomit.' Her eyes glazed over with the pain of the memory.

'*Mon Dieu.*' Thomas stared at her, open-mouthed.

'How could we have been drinking wine while Alex was…' The colour drained from her face.

'Did you go to the police? They would understand that it was an accident, surely?'

'No I didn't.' Her face twisted with pain and remorse. 'I panicked. I'm ashamed to admit that I hid the body and fled, and now I'm probably guilty of all kinds of offences.' She drew breath. 'A lot has happened, but now I'm here in France with a false identity. I'm terrified because I've been recognised by someone who saw my photo in an English paper. I'm wanted as a missing person in England. And, I've been linked to an unexplained death in Oxford.'

Thomas swallowed hard. '*Putain.*'

'I'm a fugitive, on the run, and I don't know what to do. To make matters worse, I've written a book called *The Humble Pawn*, telling the truth about what actually happened, and now it turns out to be a bestseller. I wrote it using a pseudonym, but now everyone knows it was me,' she wailed. 'What on earth am I going to do?'

'It could be worse, Céline. You didn't murder him, it was an accident. And, presumably, you have two witnesses who will testify in your favour.'

'I'm scared, truly scared.'

Thomas cupped his chin in his hands, his brow deeply furrowed. 'I'll see if I can think of anything that might help you. But, for now, I think we both need a large glass of wine.'

Chapter 26

Sophia stared at her computer screen. 'As I feared, I've got a sexually transmitted infection.'

'Me too.'

'Well, we're going to have to go to Marseillan for our antibiotics this morning, aren't we?'

Céline sighed. This is the last thing she needed today. 'Yes, I guess so,' she muttered.

'Let's go and sort ourselves out first, and then I will speak to Luca. God knows how many people he has infected.' Her face clouded over. 'How can I have been this stupid?'

'I feel exactly the same, Sophia, we should have known better, but that's all water under the bridge now.'

As the car drew into the town car park, Céline had an idea. 'Is there a shop selling art materials around here?'

'Yes, just over the road from the clinic. Why on earth do you want to go to an art shop?'

'Can we go for a coffee after we've picked up our medication, Sophia? I have something that I need to tell you.'

'Of course,' said Sophia, intrigued. 'I could certainly do with a caffeine shot after the bombshell we've just had.'

Having picked up two packs of antibiotics at the pharmacy, they made their way to a simple café. '*Deux grands crème, s'il vous plaît,*' Sophia called to the barista. 'Now, what have you got to tell me?'

'I'm worried about Moni.'

'Aren't we all?' Sophia tutted.

'She is an extremely talented artist.'

Sophia's jaw dropped with surprise. 'Well, I know she likes to doodle but…'

'No, she is truly skilful,' Céline interjected. 'I've never seen anything like the collection of drawings and paintings she showed me. She's imaginative and creative. I think she could go a long way in the art world.'

'But my sister wants her to be a doctor, or a lawyer.'

'That is the nub of the problem. Her parents obviously want what they think is best for her, to go into a highly paid, secure profession. But they are not listening to Moni.'

'Of course they are. They love her and they want her to do well…' Her eyes flashed with anger. 'How can you make assumptions and judgements about people you don't even know.'

Céline stared out of the window at the bustling street, alive with people going about their daily business. 'I'm sorry, but I have listened to what Moni has had to say. She drew a sketch of her life at home. It is pretty shocking.' She paused, considering what she should say next. 'She drew her father raising his hand towards her mother.'

Sophia gasped. 'I have had my suspicions for a while. Sylvie has become withdrawn, cagey about her relationship. But I didn't know he hit her. But what has this got to do with Monique?'

'Living in a house with warring parents is, at best, upsetting, and can often be extremely damaging for an adolescent child. Moni believes it is all her fault. The arguments are always about her.'

'Poor Moni,' Sophia said, suddenly realising the folly of her words. 'But thankfully she's with us now, so everything will be okay.'

'Do you really think so? If only life were that simple.'

'So, what do you expect me to do?'

'I think you should look at Moni's portfolio so that you can see with your own eyes how talented your niece is. Then you should talk to your sister. Moni doesn't want to be a doctor, or a lawyer, she wants to study art. If her parents realised the true potential of their daughter, then perhaps they would support her ambition. They should be very proud of Monique.'

Sophia lifted her steaming coffee to her lips, leaving a red smudge on the rim of her cup. 'You might have a point, Céline. You really think Moni has true potential?'

'I do,' Céline affirmed. 'I think she will enjoy showing you her incredible artwork. It is totally unique, exciting and innovative; she is super talented. Is it okay if I just slip over the road to the shop while you're finishing your coffee?'

'*Oui*,' she muttered.

Céline scanned the wide range of paints, paper and brushes that were attractively displayed in the tiny shop, piled high with everything an artist could possibly ever need or want. After browsing the enticing display, she carefully selected some tubes of acrylic paint, a palette knife, brushes of different thicknesses, and a couple of boards. As an afterthought, she also chose a drawing pad and a variety of pencils for sketching. Satisfied, she walked back to the coffee shop, weighed down by her purchases. There she found Sophia, still sipping the cold remnants of coffee from the bottom of her cup.

Céline smiled. 'I'll get two more coffees and a pastry. I fancy a *Jésuite*.'

Cupping her coffee in both hands, she glanced at Sophia, who now looked rather uncomfortable.

'How could I have not seen this coming? I see my sister frequently and she has never confided in me. And the worst thing is, I have never asked her if she is okay, even though, in my heart of hearts, I knew she wasn't.'

'Sometimes we get so immersed in our own lives that we don't look up.'

'I feel I've let Sylvie down.'

'Sophia, you are helping her by kindly taking in Moni. It will give them some breathing space. If you can convince Sylvie that they should listen to their daughter, trust her, and support her ambition to study art. Moni will be thrilled, it might save a lot of heartache, and it might also solve some of the problems in their marriage.'

'I think you're right, Céline. I'm so scatty that I often don't notice what's right in front of my nose. I'm sorry if I was a bit harsh earlier.'

Céline smiled benevolently. 'That's okay. So, you'll ask Moni to show you her portfolio?'

'Yes, of course. I can't wait to see her work, and from what you've said, it's going to be a pleasant surprise.'

'And you'll talk with Sylvie?'

'I promise I will, as soon as I possibly can.'

'Okay, shall we say this gift of art materials is from us both? Moni would be delighted if she knew she had your support, Sophia.'

'That's a great idea, and thank you, but I must give you some money towards it.'

'No need,' she insisted. 'Will you also talk to Luca?'

'I will. It won't be an easy conversation, but we must all face reality.'

***

'Hi, Céline, good to see you,' said Thomas, opening the front door wide to let her in.

'Thanks,' she said, furtively looking around. 'Have you talked to Nathalie about this?'

'I did, Céline, because we tell each other everything, but I know she will be discreet. I hope that is okay with you?'

'Of course, and I'm sorry I've had to bother you. You must still be reeling from the shock of Pierre's suicide.'

'I am, but his untimely death has made me realise that life is precious. It's important to talk with each other and to listen. And, of course, to help one another, which is where you come in.' He took a deep breath. 'It was just a well-intentioned birthday treat that went horribly wrong. Accidents happen. But...' He paused, looking into her eyes. 'I think you've made a grave mistake by not telling the police. To hide the body and run was reckless and, I'm sorry to say this, cowardly.'

'I know, Thomas. I was wrong.' She steepled her fingers. 'I still can't believe how cold-hearted and calculating I was.'

'We all make mistakes, but I fear this is one you might live to regret. I know you're not a bad person, you are kind and good. And I want to help you... My gut feeling is that you should go to the authorities as soon as possible, turn yourself in, and confess everything. If they realise it was an accident, the courts might be lenient.'

'You are right, I have already decided that I must go back to England and face the music, but before I do, I need time to sort out my affairs and plan my next steps.'

'I think I can help you. I have a friend, Leo, who owns the oyster shack in Marseillan. He owes me a favour or two. Shall I ask him if he could give you a temporary job, no questions asked? I'm afraid it probably won't be for more than a few weeks, but it will buy you some time.'

'That would be great, although I've not worked in a restaurant before.'

'I think that is the least of your problems,' he said, with a wry smile.

'I can't thank you enough, Thomas.'

'Well, perhaps you can treat me to a plate of oysters and a glass of Sauvignon blanc at the shack one day soon?'

'It's a deal.'

'Okay, I'll get onto that today, and, if all goes well, you can start work there before the end of the week.'

As Céline walked back along the perimeter of the field towards the old house, she felt overcome by sadness. She had grown to love her work here and she would miss Sophia and Pascal. And Luca. He had become an important part of her daily routine, and she had become very fond of him. She didn't feel that he had used her simply for sex, it had become so much more. And what would become of Monique? As she quickened her step, she strengthened her resolve to put things right.

The next morning, Monique was surprised to be greeted by Céline and Sophia.

'Are you both teaching me today?' she asked, throwing Sophia a puzzled glance.

'*Ma chérie*, Céline has been telling me about your amazing artwork. I would love to see your pictures.'

'Why?' asked Monique doubtfully.

'I just want to see how talented my niece really is.'

'Well, I suppose so, they're not that great though.' She reluctantly opened her large folder and randomly spread the pieces of art across the table.

'*Bien*.' Sophia cast her eyes across each drawing and painting, pausing to study the intricate detail of each piece. '*Ooh la la*, these are…'

Monique glanced nervously from Céline to Sophia. 'What do you think? Do you like them?'

'Do I like them, Moni? This is an extraordinary collection.'

'Extraordinary, as in odd?'

Sophia beamed from ear to ear. 'No.' She laughed. 'I mean absolutely outstanding. I'm lost for words.'

Monique's shoulders visibly relaxed. 'Do you really mean it, Sophia? You're not just saying that to make me feel better?'

Sophia looked once again at the artwork. 'You have remarkable talent, Moni. You've been hiding your light under a bushel... I had no idea.'

'I'm pleased you like them,' Monique said shyly.

Suddenly, Sophia's eyes were drawn to a sketch, half covered by the pink manilla folder. She plucked it from the table, and her face darkened. She studied the image of her sister cowering from the outstretched hand of her husband. '*Mon Dieu.*' She turned her attention to the image of a young adolescent on the floor, her back against the wall, knees bent, her head bowed, surrounded by screwed-up drawings and paintings. She drew her fingers roughly through her hair. 'I have an important phone call to make, but before I do...' She cupped Monique's cheeks with the open palm of each hand. '*Ma belle*, I am so proud that you are my niece. You will be famous one day.' With that, she turned tail and marched out of the room.

Monique turned towards Céline. 'Wow! I think Sophia quite liked my work... But I hope I haven't ruined everything by letting her see the drawing of my life at home.'

'She was blown away by your talent, Moni, and I think it is good that she saw that picture. You never know, it might make all the difference. Oh, I nearly forgot,' she said, handing Monique a large bag. 'Sophia and I bought these to encourage you to do more art while you're here.'

Monique's dark eyes glittered with pleasure as she lovingly took out each item and placed it on the table in front of her. 'I can't believe it. No one has ever done this for me before.' She gently stroked the rippled surface of the white board. 'Perfect for painting with acrylics. How did you know?'

'The power of Google,' she answered.

'You're not leaving, are you, Céline?' Monique asked anxiously. 'I don't know why, but this feels rather final? Please say you're not going.'

Céline looked away. 'I'm afraid I am. I never intended to stay here longer than a few weeks, and it is time for me to move on. I've really enjoyed working with you, and if I had half your talent, I would be bursting with pride.'

'But you have been the only person who has listened to me... I mean really listened.'

Céline looked at the young vulnerable woman in front of her. 'Now that Sophia has recognised your talent, and caught a glimpse of what life is like for you at home, I think everything might change for the better.'

Monique looked doubtful. 'Are you leaving because of the photo in the newspaper? I won't say anything, I promise,' she said, her bottom lip quivering.

Céline averted her eyes.

'You haven't answered me. Is it because of the photo?'

'Partly, yes. There are certain things in my past that I can't share, and I have to ask you if you can keep any thoughts you may have to yourself. I'm sorry to place such a heavy burden on your young shoulders. I don't think I'm being fair to be honest, but I have no choice. I'm sorry.'

Monique stared at Céline for an unnervingly long time. 'I want you to have this,' she said, reaching down to select a drawing from her portfolio. 'It is the sketch I made of you a few weeks ago.'

Céline gazed at her portrait. It was an extraordinary likeness: it was as if she was looking at her own reflection in the mirror. The features, shape and definition of her face were all perfectly portrayed. The shading on her left cheek was striking. But, as she studied the sketch more closely, her attention was drawn to something unusual, something quite distinct. Each eye had been divided in the centre by a thin horizontal line. Above the line, the pupils were bright and alert. Below the line, they were cloudy and opaque, the pupils obscured.

'I hope I've done you justice,' Monique remarked.

Céline remained silent, staring at the sketch in front of her.

'I've tried to capture your open, kind and wise features, but your eyes give you away. They tell me that you are hiding a dark secret. It is like you've pulled up the drawbridge, locked yourself away, and you won't let anyone in.'

Céline opened and closed her mouth, lost for words.

Monique turned the sketch towards herself and scribbled her signature. And something else. She slid the paper across the table to Céline. 'I have named my sketch *Queen in the Shadows*.' She locked eyes with Céline. 'You can't run away forever.'

'I don't know what to say, Moni. You have the power to see what lies beneath the surface. You touch my soul.'

She paused. 'Thank you for the sketch, I will treasure it. You never know, it may be worth a fortune when you are rich and famous,' she added, the corner of her lips twitching into a smile.

'Céline, you have absolutely no need to worry. I'm good at keeping secrets,' she said, tracing the line of her closed lips with her index finger and thumb. 'And please don't be sorry, you have given me the confidence to believe in myself. I'll never forget you.' Tears began to flow freely down her face. 'I will miss you.'

Chapter 27

The sharp bitterness of the dark syrupy coffee lodged in her throat.

'Please don't go.' His dark-brown eyes expressed raw emotion, his sentiments simple. 'I need you.'

'You have to understand, I was never going to stay for long.'

Luca cupped both her hands in his. 'What can I do to make you stay? I'll do anything.'

Céline gently stroked the sandpapery stubble of his unshaven cheek. 'My mind is made up. Nothing you say or do will change that.' She peered at him through the mistiness of her tears. 'You are special, Luca, I will always cherish our time together.' She paused. 'But I want you to do one last thing for me.'

He pushed away the thick blanket of hair that fell across his face. 'For you, anything.'

'Be open with the doctor and tell him about all your conquests. I know you didn't mean to cause harm, but it is very important that everyone is checked and treated.'

His eyes flashed with annoyance. 'I can't remember them all,' he muttered. 'And anyway, shouldn't people take personal responsibility? What time period are we talking about?'

'I don't think it's quite that simple… And I have no idea about the time frame, but I'm sure the doctor will advise you.'

'*Putain*. We can't spend our last evening together talking about problems,' he said gruffly. 'I will do as you ask, Céline. I will sort this out.'

'Thanks, Luca. It is important that you do.'

The chair legs scraped on the tiles as he rose and strode over to the dresser. 'I have a gift for you.'

Opening the drawer, he pulled out a small package carefully wrapped in brown paper and tied up with string. Céline slowly peeled away the thick wrapping, to reveal a shallow wooden box. On the lid, an intricate pattern cut deep into the grain, complimenting the rich swirls of colour in the wood. She lifted the box towards her face, closed her eyes, and inhaled the rich scent of seasoned wood and perfumed oil.

'I carved it myself, using the wood of dried vine roots,' he said proudly.

She opened the lid, attached by a cunningly designed dowel hinge. Nestled in the cushioned lining lay a thin band of burnished gold. 'I don't know what to say, Luca. This is such a beautiful gift.' Stroking the smooth surface of the ring, her brow creased with concern. 'You know I can't marry you,' she mumbled nervously.

Luca chuckled. 'I'm not asking you to marry me. This is a traditional friendship band. It has been in my family for generations, and I would like you to have it. Will you wear it and remember me?' He slipped the band onto the middle finger of her right hand and stood back to admire it. 'Gold suits you.'

Céline gazed at the ring, which fitted snugly on her finger. 'Are you sure? It's a family heirloom. Perhaps you should give it to the woman you eventually settle down with?' she mused.

'I don't think that will ever happen. No, I want you to have it.'

'In that case, I will wear it with pride. And thank you.' She turned her attention to the wooden box. 'And this will always remind me of you. You have created this magnificent casket using the earth's natural resources, and you are an earthy creature of the land.'

Luca raised his eyebrows quizzically. *'Je ne comprends pas.'*

'It's too hard to explain, Luca,' she said, with a smile.

They spent the evening eating simple country fare, drinking a couple of glasses of a rare vintage wine that Luca had saved for a special occasion, and they reminisced about the special times they had enjoyed together. All too soon it was time to say their sad farewells.

'You will always be in my heart, Céline.' After one last lingering kiss, she turned and disappeared into the night.

***

Céline sat on her bed, gazing out of the window at the dawn sky, etched with red and gold. She sighed as wave upon wave of exhaustion shuddered through her body.

She had always felt unsettled by change, but leaving the old house, and all her new-found friends, was harder than she had anticipated. She had been overcome by sadness saying goodbye to Luca. She knew she was falling in love with him, and, if things had been different, they would still be together. She had never before, and she would never again, meet anyone like Luca: a wild free-thinker, a dynamic lover, a person at one with nature. But it was not to be.

She smiled. Sophia and Pascal seemed to have rekindled their marriage during the last few weeks. Céline couldn't help but notice the discreet loving glances passing between them, small signs of physical affection, a fleeting kiss, or a cuddle; they laughed and chatted together. It would probably take longer to fully repair the cracks, but they had certainly turned a corner.

Her thoughts turned to Monique. Sophia had it within her power to talk to her sister and perhaps help her to realise that Moni is creative and driven to pursue the arts. Maybe, just maybe, everything would turn out for the best for the young woman, and her parents. Monique had unique insight and a wise head on her shoulders. She would go far. She had certainly seen through Céline's facade: *You can't run away forever*. How right she was.

Mr Isaac Goldmann had become a regular feature in Céline's daily life. She had learnt so much about the atrocities of war, and the importance of humility, kindness and resilience. She would probably never know his fate, but she felt honoured to have been able to catch a glimpse into his world. Céline was pleased that she had been able to pass the journal on to Thomas. It was incredible that the driver who rescued Isaac from almost certain death in Marseille was none other than his father's best friend, Thomas Debois: Thomas's namesake. She had faith that he would find a suitable resting place for the journal, Isaac Goldmann's words had the potential to bring the dusty history books to life.

She had become good friends with Thomas and Nathalie. They lived a frugal life, and they both worked hard to put food on the table for their young family. Their way of living on the commune was hard but they were surrounded by a network of support, in stark contrast to the more formal routine and atmosphere in the old house.

And what of Gaston, and the tragic loss of his son, Pierre? He had been brave to share his wise words with the commune after his son took his own life. Gaston talked about the sanctity of life and how we should make the most of each and every day: life is precious. He shared his feelings about his son's sexuality, and how we must value and respect everyone for who they are. He truly loved his son.

Her thoughts were interrupted by Sophia calling from the kitchen. 'Breakfast is ready. You'd better be quick because Thomas will be here soon.'

She was greeted by Sophia and Pascal, smiling conspiratorially at one another. 'We have some news,' said Pascal, beaming from ear to ear.

Céline looked from one to the other. 'Well? Don't keep me in suspense.'

'We've decided we would like to have a child, so we have registered for adoption. The process might take a while, but we feel that we are ready to start a family.'

Céline drew breath. 'How exciting...' She engulfed them both in her outstretched arms. 'Wonderful news!'

Sophia gazed at the smiling face of her husband. 'I can't believe we're actually going to do this.' Pascal stroked her hair lovingly. 'It will be the start of a new era, *ma chérie*.' He chuckled. 'And the end of peace and quiet for years to come!'

'I know this special child will be loved by everyone!' added Céline.

After breakfast, a car drew up on the long gravel drive. Pascal collected all her luggage and squashed it into the boot. She warmly embraced Sophia and Pascal. 'À *bientôt, j'espère*,' she said, as she climbed into the front seat of the car, clutching her rucksack containing her documents and valuables.

The time had come to say goodbye and move on to pastures new.

Chapter 28

The bedroom was small and pokey, and the bed squeaked. She slumped on the wooden chair in front of the shuttered window and stared into space. Céline had been at the oyster shack for two weeks, and she had fallen into a comfortable daily routine. She started the day with a simple breakfast which she prepared in the kitchen and ate in her room. At eleven o'clock her shift began, setting up the tables and polishing the wine glasses. At about midday customers trickled in: individuals, business men and women dressed in smart suits, entertaining their clients, and, at weekends, large family groups gathered to enjoy a feast of *coquillages et crustacés* – shellfish and crustaceans. Although the restaurant was popular, it was now low season and the tourists had left, leaving only the locals, and a few roving business men. Her shifts were bustling but never too busy, and the restaurant only opened its doors at lunchtime.

Céline enjoyed her work. The quality of the food was excellent, and the customers usually left with a full tummy and a wide smile. She particularly enjoyed the atmosphere at the weekends, watching families, often spanning generations – tiny babies to great-grandparents

– immersed in lively conversation, young children busily slurping the upturned oysters into their open mouths. The gentle hubbub of conversation rose and fell, interspersed by laughter and silence, everyone content. A *Brasucade* was offered every day: vine roots burnt under a generous tray of mussels, the smoke curling up towards the pastel-blue autumnal sky. The aroma was intoxicating.

Leo, the owner of the oyster shack, was a friendly man in his early sixties. His hair was jet black, offset with flecks of silver. His face an open book, his skin like leather. He charmed everyone with his sharp wit and his beguiling smile. He left England and moved to France in his early twenties, after becoming disenchanted with his homeland. He was quick to set up a small business selling oysters on the banks of the Étang *de Thau*. The business grew organically until he had accumulated enough custom and funds to set up a small oyster shack. He had an imaginative mind brimming over with innovative ideas. Whoever would have thought of serving cooked oysters with melted chocolate as a desert? He liaised with the fishermen on their trawlers and local wine producers to source the very best of everything, and before long he had a highly successful restaurant with an excellent reputation.

The winter months were always quiet and Leo used this time productively to experiment with new recipes and source new and exciting ingredients to expand his repertoire. He had recently introduced *tielle sétoise* to the menu. The family recipe for *tielle* had been passed down from Italian immigrant fisherman to the passionate bakers of *Sète*. It was originally known as a poor man's pie but was now seen as a gastronomic delight. The essential ingredients of the *tielle* are octopus or squid and tomatoes, all mixed into a rich filling and topped with a generous layer of pastry. They were extremely popular with the customers, and every day dozens of steaming pies flew straight from the oven to the plate.

Céline enjoyed Leo's company. He always insisted on high-quality service – a hard taskmaster – but he was fair and honest, and always quick to compliment good, attentive service. Céline relished her conversations with him. She had spoken French continuously for weeks, and although her spoken language had improved, she found it refreshing and relaxing to speak in English. She also relished the company of someone who wasn't trying to seduce her.

Her shift finished at about three o'clock, when she had cleared the last table and made sure that everything was shipshape and ready for the next day. Then she had the rest of the day to herself.

This particular afternoon, after the last customer had left the restaurant, Leo called her into the office. Céline sighed. She knew what was coming. He invited her to sit down, smiling apologetically. He explained that her work in the restaurant had been exemplary, but unfortunately he had no choice, he would have to let her go. He gave her three weeks' notice and a month's salary in advance. 'I would hang on to you if I could, Céline. You're one of the best, the customers love you and we always get good tips when you're on duty. But unfortunately it's too quiet in the winter months to warrant so many staff on the payroll. So, last in, first out, I'm afraid.'

Céline thanked Leo for his kindness and generosity, assuring him that she understood his predicament, and that she had always known that it would only be a short-term arrangement. He engulfed her in his arms, the wool of his fisherman's jumper rough against her cheek. 'It has been a pleasure,' he said, giving her a reassuring squeeze. 'But it isn't over yet. We still have the joy of your company for another three weeks! And if I can help you to find another job locally, then give me a shout.'

***

She stared blankly at the stained porcelain bowl, her thin frame contorting with pain and exhaustion. Heaving over and over again, she tasted the sour bile, bitter on her tongue. She roughly pulled back the damp strands of hair from her face, breathing in the distinctive and acidic smell of vomit.

She glanced at her watch. It was ten to eleven and she was due to start work at eleven o'clock. She hurriedly splashed cold water on her face and brushed her teeth, hoping that the peppermint flavour of her toothpaste would mask the overwhelming smell of sickness.

'God, Céline, you look terrible...' Leo stared at her in horror. 'You're as white as a sheet,' he said, taking her by the arm and gently sitting her down on one of the high stools in front of the bar. 'I'll get you some water.'

Céline groaned. She had two and half weeks of work

left, and the last thing she needed was to be ill. She had so much to think about and to do before she left Marseillan.

'You haven't looked well for a few days now. I'll will ring Daniel Lacroix. He's a friend of mine and a really good doctor. He'll be able to help you.'

'Okay, thanks. I must admit, I don't feel great,' Céline conceded, 'although maybe I'll be better tomorrow.'

Leo disappeared into the office, returning a few minutes later. 'He'll see you this afternoon. He's making a few house calls nearby, so he'll call in around two o'clock. How does that sound?'

Céline smiled weakly. 'Thanks, Leo, although I'm sure he's got patients on his list with more serious complaints than mine.'

'I think it's important that you are seen by a medical professional. Apart from anything else, I want reassurance that it is not a duff oyster or *bulot* that has made you sick.' He paused. 'Now, we are rather short-staffed today but if you want to take some time out, I'm sure we can manage.'

'I'll be fine,' she said resolutely. She struggled through the rest of the shift, feeling drained and weak, and fully aware of Leo watching her like a hawk. She smiled at him, grateful for his kind concern and unwavering support, even though she was just temporary.

Turning down the offer of a bite to eat, Céline returned to her room, grateful for some peace and quiet, relieved that she was feeling a little better. She lay on her bed, and soon her eyes closed and she sank into a restless sleep.

At exactly two o'clock there was a knock on her bedroom door. She opened her eyes sleepily. A gentleman with a kindly face and eyes that twinkled behind red-framed glasses popped his head round the door. '*Bonjour, madame.* I am Dr Lacroix. Is it okay that I come in?' he asked in broken English.

'Of course,' she mumbled.

'Now, how can I help you?'

'Well, I've been feeling a bit rough recently. I've been sick a few times, and I feel rather weak and wobbly.'

'Oh dear. Let me have a look at you.'

Céline was surprised by how thoroughly the doctor examined her. 'Is everything okay? It's only a sickness bug, isn't it?'

He didn't answer but continued to do various tests, temperature, blood pressure, a pelvic examination, and he asked for a urine sample. Eventually, he sat on the wooden chair by her bed. 'Well I'm pleased to tell you that you are fit and healthy.'

'Phew,' she said. 'That's a relief… not that I was really panicking about having a horrible illness or anything.'

'I'm sorry that you've been feeling nauseous in the mornings though,' he continued. 'Although you feel poorly now, you should feel a lot better during the second trimester.'

Céline gasped.

'It's quite normal to experience morning sickness in the first three months,' he said, trying to reassure her.

Céline stared at him, open-mouthed. 'What are you saying?'

'You're having a baby.' The doctor peered over his glasses. 'You didn't know?'

'But it's not possible.'

'Take a deep breath, Céline, this has obviously come as rather a shock,' he said gently. 'Why don't you think it's possible?'

'My ex-husband… I thought I was unable to conceive. We tried for years…'

'Sometimes there is no rhyme or reason, these things just happen. Perhaps it was your ex who was infertile?'

Céline pushed any thoughts she had about her ex-husband, Alex, to the back of her mind. She reached under the duvet and gently stroked her belly. 'I can't believe it. You mean I'm actually going to have a baby?'

'Yes, it's true.'

It was the last thing she expected, and Céline couldn't suppress a smile.

Chapter 29

Sometimes when your hen won't lay, you just have to change the cock.

Céline gave a wry smile as she recalled the tale of an old family friend, a chicken farmer. His words, ironically, resonated with her. The lingering smell of disinfectant and aftershave hung in the air long after Dr Lacroix had gone, and she was left deep in thought. She had to pinch herself to believe that what the wise doctor had told her was actually true.

She had wanted to have a baby for many years, but, after the initial euphoria, harsh reality hit her like a ton of bricks. Questions spun around in her head, like clothes in a washing machine: *Who is the father? Is it Luca, or could it be...?* Her heart started to race. *No, it has to be Luca. Doesn't it? Should I tell him?*

Her mind was made up. She wouldn't tell Luca, it would be her secret. But she would have to move quickly, the prospect of a baby arriving in a few months' time sharpened her mind. She must return to England and confess everything. Perhaps the courts would be lenient, given the fact that Alex's death was an accident. She had written her memoir and it had become a bestseller. And now she was expecting a baby.

Her heart fluttered with terror and excitement in equal measure. The prospect of being single and alone with a young baby was daunting. She knew that she would have to muster all her strength and resilience for the next few weeks and months.

The next day after work, she had a visitor. She opened the front door to find Thomas towering over her. He smiled brightly. 'Céline, it's a sunny day. Do you fancy some lunch?'

'What a lovely surprise. I haven't got anything else in my diary,' she said, shrugging her shoulders. 'Why not?'

'The kids are at school and I've got a couple of hours to spare. Nathalie is sorry that she couldn't come today, she hears children read in Sammy's class every Tuesday. There's a great restaurant just down the road, shall we go there? It's just a short walk away.'

'Yes, let's. I'll just get my things.' She threw her cashmere wrap round her shoulders and together they strode towards Le Bistro.

'*Bonjour, Monsieur Thomas, allez-y.*' The young waitress led them to a table by the window and balanced a black board by the side of the table. '*Voilà,*' she said, flamboyantly waving her arms in the air.

'*Ooh la la, coq au vin,* my favourite. Everything is freshly prepared on site by *madame*, so it will be very tasty.'

Céline put her hand over her mouth to conceal her amusement. She couldn't help but think about the obvious connection between the *menu du jour* and the tale that the old chicken farmer had told her.

'What wine shall we have? Do you fancy red, white or rosé? Personally, I like a drop of red to complement *coq au vin*. They do have some good house wines here.'

'I'll stick to a soft drink today. I think I'll have a *citron pressé*, please.'

'That's not like you,' Thomas remarked, twitching his mouth sideways. 'Are you ill? You do look rather pale.'

'I'm fine thanks, Thomas, just a bit tired,' she said, her words tumbling out quickly. 'And I didn't sleep well last night.'

'*D'accord*,' he said, staring at her with interest. 'How's it all going? I'm sure Leo is looking after you well?'

'I'm really enjoying the work in the restaurant. But, to be honest, I wouldn't care if I never saw another oyster again in my entire life.'

Thomas laughed. 'Leo serves the best *coquillage* this side of Paris. If anyone could tempt you, he could...'

Céline began to feel queasy at the very thought of a raw oyster, but she looked forward to a comforting casserole.

'I'm glad you like the work. How is everything else?'

'Well I don't want to seem ungrateful, but the room is really cold. I do enjoy Leo's company, but I don't have many friends, and I can't see that changing because I'm only here for another two weeks.'

'Oh no. Why?'

'They don't need me in the restaurant because it's not busy enough.' She glanced at Thomas's crestfallen face. 'Don't worry, I always knew I wasn't going to be here for long.'

'Oh dear. What are your plans?'

'I haven't had a chance to think. To be honest, I haven't been feeling myself lately,' she said, instantly regretting her words.

'Tell me, Céline, what's wrong? Have you seen the doctor?'

She blushed. 'Yes, I saw Dr Lacroix yesterday, and there's nothing to worry about.' She knew she mustn't tell Thomas the truth, because the news would almost certainly spread to the rest of the commune, and to Luca.

'Alright, Céline, but please promise me you'll look after yourself. The winter is coming, and even though we're on the Mediterranean coast, we get the cold winds from the mountains. You need to eat good food and wrap up warmly. But where will you go after this? You can always stay with us if you get desperate.'

'That's very kind of you, but I have to move on. I must return to England sooner rather than later.' She clenched her hands together. 'But there are so many barriers in the way. I don't have a passport, my ID is fake, and I'm not prepared to pay people smugglers.'

'Why don't you go to the British consulate in Marseille, and tell them the whole story? They might be able to repatriate you. It's all very complicated, way beyond my understanding, but I'm sure they could help.'

'I did wonder if that might be possible,' she mused. 'I have friends in Marseille, I could give them a call.'

'Good idea, and, for the record, I think you're wise to own up to everything. You never know, things might turn out well for you.'

'Or I could go to prison,' she said gruffly.

'Well, you'll never find out if you keep running.' He leaned in towards her and brushed her cheek lightly with the tips of his fingers. 'Poor you, Céline, you look totally exhausted.'

'Nothing that a couple of good nights' sleep won't sort out.'

Thomas studied her face. 'Okay, so how can I help you?'

'I'm not sure…'

'Why don't I drive you to Marseille, and take you to your friend's house?'

'That would be amazing, but are you sure? It's a long drive…'

'No problem, Céline, I'm happy to help in any way that I can. So it's settled then?'

She smiled and gratefully accepted his kind offer.

'And, to change the subject, I took Isaac Goldmann's journal to our local museum. A historian has been assigned to do some research into Isaac's family history and ancestry. Perhaps he will discover what actually happened to Isaac; whether he escaped, or if he was captured and imprisoned… or worse. I'm curious to find out more about his fate… I really didn't know I liked history this much.'

'Great news! Isaac's journal finished so abruptly, and many questions were left unanswered.'

'It may take time, but I feel sure that we will eventually find out a lot more about Isaac Goldmann and his life.'

**

The van hurtled up the motorway towards Marseille, bottles of wine clinking rhythmically in the back.

'*Putain*. There are so many speed cameras along the A9, I must pay attention.'

Céline glanced at the speedometer, which was wavering at just over the 120 kilometre mark. 'What is the speed limit here?'

'In good conditions it's 130, so we're within the limit. I think it will take about three hours to get there, depending on the traffic, of course. Just relax and enjoy the scenery, we're following the coastal route all the way, so we'll have some beautiful views of the Med.'

Céline took a deep breath and realised that she felt anything but relaxed. She had been sorry to leave the old house, and her life there, behind. Today, she had left the oyster shack just as she was beginning to settle into the routine. And, on top of all this, she was pregnant. Change always unsettled her, and she was frightened about the future and what she would have to face. She stared gloomily out of the window, watching as the vast expanse of countryside passed by in a blur.

'Everything will be okay, Céline, you'll see,' Thomas said, as if he could read her mind.

Céline sighed. If only she could share just a fraction of his optimism.

'Just take one step at a time.' He reached over to the glovebox, pulled out a large packet of sweets, and thrust it carelessly onto her lap. 'Fancy a mint? When I'm stressed, I find eating helps.'

She gazed affectionately at her friend. Thomas's

eyes were fixed on the road, his tanned face creased in concentration. His broad shoulders were hunched over the wheel, revealing a round greasy patch above him, where his hair usually brushed the roof. His limbs were so ridiculously long that he almost had to fold himself double to squeeze into the driving well. She felt safe with him. He was kind and capable, and he always knew what to do for the best. She would miss Thomas, his friendly banter, his wise words and his wicked sense of humour.

She closed her eyes, listening to the steady hum of the engine, and, before long, she fell into a fitful sleep, her head lolling from one side to the other.

'Céline, wake up, we're just coming up to the outskirts of Marseille. I think you told me that your friends live in the Old Port?'

'Yes, Jacques and Nicole live in a flat by the marina,' she muttered, rubbing the left side of her neck.

'I'm glad you had a sleep. The traffic has been horrendous, and it has taken much longer than I thought. Thankfully, we're only about five minutes away. Can you set the satnav?'

'Oh dear, I'm sorry I slept for so long.'

'*Ce n'est pas grave.* Are you going to tell your friends what is going on?'

'Yes, I think I owe them an explanation, they have been very kind to me.'

'Would it be easier if I recounted your circumstances to Jacques and Nicole? Your French is good, but mine is better,' he said, turning to look at her, his eyes glittering.

'Would you really do that for me, Thomas? Thank you.'

The only piece of information Céline chose not to share was her pregnancy. She reached down and gently stroked her belly.

She looked out of the window as they arrived in the Old Port. Everything looked different now with the onset of winter. Only a few yachts remained in the water, the other boats were cradled in the boatyard, just visible across the bay. The pavements were quieter now and some of the shops were closed and shuttered, prepared for the inevitable storms of winter. Céline took some comfort in the familiarity of the area, and the memories she had of meeting Nicole in the café, her style and her chic manner. "I do love *coquillage*, but there is nothing like *bouillabaisse*, especially when it is made locally in Marseille." She turned to watch the boats bobbing about in the bay, and listened as the halliards beat against the masts. She pictured *Carpe Diem* and the blissful cruise she had enjoyed with Jacques, blushing at the memory of the passionate encounter they had had on the foredeck... Only to be disturbed by the ringing of the bell, signalling a plump bass on the end of the line. She wished she was meeting her friends under happier circumstances.

Jacques and Nicole warmly welcomed them both into their chic waterside apartment and offered them a large glass of Chardonnay. '*Bienvenue, mes amis.*'

Thomas wasted no time. He recounted the long painful events of Céline's life. As the story unfolded, the conversation was frequently interrupted by softly spoken swear words: *putain… merde.* Céline listened, understanding most of the conversation, but not all of it. Eventually, Thomas paused. All eyes fixed on Céline. She bowed her head, embarrassed and ashamed of how dishonest she had been to the very people who had helped her. She could feel her heart beating hard against her ribcage. She was unsure about the reception she would get.

But she need not have feared.

'My poor darling, how you must have suffered,' Nicole soothed.

Chapter 30

'My name is Libby Wilkinson.'

'I am the missing person from Oxford.'

'I am the author of *The Humble Pawn*.'

At last, it was out. She had confessed everything.

After her meeting at the British consulate, Céline felt like a weight had been lifted from her shoulders. She was to return to the consulate the next day to pick up her temporary paperwork and to take an early evening flight from Marseille to Heathrow.

Jacques was waiting outside the wrought-iron gates of the building in his car, ready to pick her up and take her back to the apartment for her last evening in France.

When they arrived home, Jacques led her out onto the balcony overlooking the marina and, in the distance, the iconic sight of *Château d'If* rising majestically out of the dark tempestuous Mediterranean sea. Thick grey clouds swept across the early evening sky, threatening a wild winter storm. 'I'm sure you feel as if you are in the eye of the worst imaginable storm now, Céline, but after that, the sun *will* rise again. There will be an answer.' He smiled. 'It all sounds rather poetic, doesn't it? But I mean it, Céline. I do believe that out of darkness comes the light.'

Céline gazed at him, her eyes filled with tears. 'I hope you are right, Jacques. There is so much I regret in my life, I wish I could turn back time and do everything differently.'

'We learn by our mistakes. I've made more than my fair share in life.' He raised an eyebrow. 'But we have to put it all down to experience. You are a strong woman. You have survived so much. All our experiences make us into who you are. And I'm proud to call you my friend.'

'I guess we can't change the past, but we have the power to frame the future.'

'Exactly, Céline. I couldn't have put it better myself. And that is precisely what you are doing now. And, we wouldn't have had the pleasure of meeting you if everything had been different.'

All of a sudden, horizontal sheets of rain dashed from one side of the bay to the other. '*Merde*. Time for supper, methinks,' he said, clasping her damp hand in his.

The atmosphere around the supper table was amiable but tinged with sadness. Céline had come to love France, and all the people she had met along the way. She knew it would be a wrench to leave her friends and the French shores behind.

'Once this is all over, you can always decide to settle in France. You have French blood in your family, so, I think this might make it easier to gain French citizenship,' Nicole suggested.

Céline's face briefly lit up. 'You have given me food for thought. But I have so much to sort out before I can start to plan anything beyond the next few weeks and months.'

'Always cling on to hope, Céline. I love to dream about the future…'

'Heaven help me, Nicole wants a huge mansion fit for a queen, and a large fluffy dog!' Jacques said, raising his eyes to heaven.

Everyone laughed. '*Bien sûr*,' she purred.

As the last tasty morsels of food were scraped from the plate, Céline let out a deep sigh. 'Thank you, I loved the time I spent with you both. You are friends for life and I will never forget you.'

***

Céline strained her neck to stare out of the window and catch a final glimpse of France, the country she had grown to love. She followed the rugged coastline as it carved its way inland to form the bay, marking the entrance to the Old Port of Marseille. She gazed as the vast expanse of the Mediterranean, its surface dotted with white horses, rolled relentlessly towards the coastline. As the land disappeared beneath a dense blanket of cloud, she made a solemn promise to herself. She would return to France one day. Suddenly, the darkness turned to light as the plane rose into the blue, the clouds forming a fluffy white carpet below. Rays of sunshine streamed through the window, casting an iridescent glow. At that moment, she knew.

As the aeroplane began its descent, Céline watched as the twinkling lights of London came into view: the roads impossibly busy with queues of traffic and divided by the random pathway of the Thames curling its way through the densely populated city. Her ears popped as the plane landed, the wheels touching smoothly onto the runway with a loud roar. The time had come.

The young man in passport control studied Céline's temporary paperwork with suspicion. She was hustled into Immigration, where she had to wait for over an hour. She stared at the blank walls of the office and gloom descended.

'I apologise for the wait.' A young, smartly dressed official strode into the room and sat down on a chair behind a desk. 'I've had to make a few enquiries and finalise arrangements.'

Céline looked directly at him and nodded.

'You will be met in the Arrivals lounge by two uniformed police officers. They will escort you to Oxford where you are expected to report to St Aldates Police Station. I'm afraid I don't know anything else at this stage,' he said, looking slightly puzzled. 'Is this what you are expecting?'

'Yes,' Céline replied curtly. 'May I go now?'

'Indeed you can, they are waiting for you. It shouldn't take long to collect your luggage from the pickup area.' He hesitated before adding, 'Wrap up warm, it's cold out there.'

She plucked her small suitcase, the last item circulating on the conveyor belt, and made her way to the arrivals area. A few people were still patiently waiting to collect passengers, one or two holding banners indicating their names or businesses. She glanced to her left and there they were. Two burly police officers. She strode towards them, her confident gait effectively hiding the fear that consumed her.

She pulled her coat tightly around her midriff as they left the warmth of the airport and gulped the freezing air of England. Now that she is on English soil, she must leave Céline Dupont behind. Her name is Libby Wilkinson. A light frost sparkled on the pavement as they made their way to the police car parked in the multi-storey car park. 'Cor, it's parky tonight, and these places are always extra cold and damp,' said one of the police officers. 'I'll turn the heater on and we'll soon warm up.'

The journey from London to Oxford passed in a flash, and before long they drew up outside the entrance to the police station. Céline glanced across the road to see the ornate and formidable building housing Oxford Crown Court. She knew this is where her fate would be sealed.

Overwhelmed, she was hustled into a small interrogation room. 'Is your name Libby Wilkinson?'

'Yes,' she answered.

'Before you are questioned, you must be informed of your legal rights.' Two police officers sat opposite her, a simple wooden desk separating them. Libby listened, but the words seemed to float over her head. She watched nervously as one of the officers turned on the tape recorder and gave the interview a brief introduction and context. The interview began well enough, with straightforward questions that she could answer. As it progressed, the questions became more complex and intense. Her head was foggy with exhaustion; she tried to give full and honest answers, but she was unable to focus, and she knew that every word she uttered could incriminate her, with potentially devastating consequences. 'Before I answer any more questions, I must request a lawyer.'

Disappointment registered on their faces as the tape recorder was turned off and the interview was concluded. After a lengthy wait, she was informed that she had been granted bail. She agreed to the conditions: she must reside at a named address, and report to the police station once a week until the date of the court hearing. They also kept her legal documentation.

Questions spun in her head. Where could she go? Where would she stay? She plucked her mobile phone out of her rucksack and rang Roland, a friend who lived in Oxford. She briefly outlined the situation, and he readily agreed to pick her up from the station. She sighed with relief. Roland was a good friend.

'Libby, I am really pleased to see you,' he said, sweeping her into a warm embrace. 'I'll just confirm my address with reception, and then we will be on our way. I bet you're exhausted aren't you, my poor darling?'

Libby melted into his arms, weak from the challenges she had faced in the last few hours. He took her hand and placed it in the crook of his arm. 'You'll feel better after a good night's sleep.'

She stared out of the window as the houses on either side of Banbury Road passed them by, and they arrived in Summertown. The restaurants were alive with customers, but the shops had all closed for the night. Roland took a right turn and negotiated the narrow road, with cars parked either side until he turned into the gravel driveway of an Elizabethan semi-detached house. 'Eloise decided to have an early night, but she's looking forward to seeing you tomorrow. Can I get you anything? A cuppa or a nightcap maybe?'

'No thanks, Roly. I think I'll be asleep before my head touches the pillow. I really can't thank you enough.'

***

As they wandered through Christchurch meadow, the immaculate green lawns, marked out for cricket in the summer months, were now blanketed with a thin white layer of frost, individual particles glittering like diamonds in the pale winter sun. The university buildings, steeped in history, rose from the immaculate gardens, magnificent in their architectural splendour. As they walked along the treelined avenue towards the river, they reminisced about times gone by. So much water had passed under the bridge since their last meeting in the university parks, when Roland had given her advice on how to disappear without a trace. He had been a true friend and confidant that day, and she had followed his instructions to the letter.

She told him of her adventures in Salcombe and her escape to France. Roly listened attentively, occasionally pausing to sweep back an unruly mop of curls from his face. She described her adventures in Marseille and later working in a vineyard in the southwest. 'I can't believe it. I simply can't believe it,' he exclaimed. He stopped in his tracks when she recounted her discovery of the journal of Mr Isaac Goldmann, detailing his escape from the round-up of the Jews in Marseille during the Second World War. 'Fascinating,' he muttered. 'What a find, Libby.'

As the river came into view, they paused to study a row of houseboats, some immaculate, others littered with fallen leaves and dilapidated. She breathed in the smoke rising from the chimney pipes, the smell instantly conjuring up images of her childhood.

She described life in the vineyard, her friendship with Pascal and Sophia, and her passionate liaison with Luca. 'Well, Libby, I like the sound of Luca,' he said, his eyes twinkling with pleasure. 'He sounds just my sort of bloke!' She recounted the moment when she was finally discovered as a missing person from Oxford. And the author of a book called *The Humble Pawn*.

'I've read the book, Libby, it is brilliant, pure genius…'

'I was amazed when I saw the extract from *The Sunday Times*. It's an international bestseller,' Libby said in surprise.

He peered at her over his half-rimmed spectacles. 'It is a literary masterpiece. I'm proud to know you. Oh, and by the way, can I share the millions of pounds you'll receive in royalties?'

Libby giggled. 'Anyway, getting back to the story, I had to leave the vineyard in a hurry and a friend found me temporary work in an oyster restaurant.'

'Oysters… I like them cooked, but I'm not so sure about raw oysters,' he said, wrinkling up his nose.

She stopped and faced Roland. 'I was employed at the restaurant for less than a month… And there is something else I need to tell you… Taking everything into account,

I came to the conclusion that the time had come for me to return to England and confess everything. I must stop hiding and face my demons. And so here I am, Roly.'

'You, Libby Wilkinson, are the bravest person I know. And who knew that you could sail single-handed and navigate across the Channel? But you mentioned something you need to tell me?'

Libby absentmindedly stroked her expanding midriff.

'Bloody hell, you're not, are you?'

Chapter 31

'I could go to prison.'

Libby was agitated and nervous. 'I have to be in court in two days, and I feel like running away,' she wailed. 'What on earth will happen? I'm expecting a baby…'

'I have asked colleagues who specialise in law and I've done extensive research on the internet. I am confident that we have the best defence lawyer, Libby,' Roland soothed. 'There is nothing more we can do now, I'm afraid, we will just have to wait.'

He glanced out of the kitchen window. 'I think it's going to be a cold hard winter.' He narrowed his eyes. 'It's only mid-December and it's already snowing.'

Libby gazed into the garden. Snowflakes blew in the air, held by the cold northerly wind, before forming a soft layer on the frosted ground. She shivered. 'It looks like the Arctic out there.'

'I think we should wander into Oxford and have a mulled wine in The Turf Tavern,' Roland said, looking across at his wife, Eloise, who was making the coffee. 'The cold weather is making me feel rather festive.' He glanced across at Libby, who looked forlorn.

'Who knows where I'll be at Christmas?' she mused.

'Come on, Libs,' Roland cajoled, 'I think you need something fortifying to warm the cockles of your heart. The Turf Tavern makes a delicious non-alcoholic highly spiced mulled wine. It isn't quite as good as the real thing,' he said, with a chuckle, 'but it is pretty good.'

'I've got things to do this morning,' Eloise said, 'but you two go, it sounds like a great idea.'

Cornmarket Street was busy with shoppers hoping to buy a few early Christmas presents. A homeless man sat outside the church on a simple stool, guitar on his knee, singing "Blowing in the Wind", his voice gravelly like Bob Dylan. His lined, gaunt face told a story of hardship and struggle. But he broke into a wide toothless grin when Roland reached deep into his pocket and threw a few coins into the empty upturned cap positioned in front of him.

Turning the corner into Broad Street, they quickened their pace as the piercingly cold air cut through their woolly coats. Libby pulled her hat down over her ears. As they approached Blackwell's bookshop on the left, they stopped in their tracks. There in the window of the double-fronted shop, was an eye-catching display made up from a single title: *The Humble Pawn*.

Libby stared at the shop window, lost for words.

'Your fame goes before you, Libby.'

She blinked in surprise. 'Is this for real? I can't believe that my book has a massive display in a famous bookshop like Blackwell's.'

'*The Humble Pawn* is very popular, it will undoubtedly be on top of everyone's Christmas list.' Roland laughed.

'You really have no idea how good your book is, have you? You should read all the five-star reviews.'

Libby took a deep breath and marched into the bookshop. 'My name is Libby Wilkinson. I am the author of *The Humble Pawn*. Would you like me to do some book signings while I'm here?'

The assistant looked at her doubtfully. 'Really?'

'Yes. I thought you might be pleased?'

'The trouble is, we can't just set up an impromptu signing, we would need to book a launch and send out formal invitations. And I'm afraid we're fully booked until the New Year.'

Libby studied the vacant face of the inexperienced shopkeeper. 'Okay, your loss. Thank you for your time.'

Just as she was leaving the shop, a teenage boy tapped her on the shoulder. 'Excuse me, Miss, would you mind signing my copy?' he asked, his eyes shining with excitement.

'Of course,' she said, turning to the shop assistant. 'Please may I borrow a pen?'

***

The queue stretched up Broad Street, everyone jostling for position. Libby sat behind a large wooden table. She took time to exchange a few words with each customer before writing a personal message in the front of each book. After a couple of hours, the queue had diminished, leaving a lone woman, positioned well back from the table.

'Would you like me to sign your book for you?' Libby asked kindly.

The young woman stared at Libby. Her dull and haunted eyes flickered, sending a deep shiver down the author's spine. She spoke in a measured voice. 'I have suffered emotional abuse at the hands of my husband for years.' She roughly shook her head. 'Words can damage you. Words can destroy you...' She swallowed hard. 'Emotional abuse often slips under the radar and goes unnoticed.' She drew her shoulders back and stretched up to her full height. 'But I tell you this. It is every bit as agonising as being physically battered.' She jutted out her jaw in defiance. 'But reading your book has given me the strength I need to break free from the cruel and callous man I married. I *will* find a better life.'

Libby reached across and cupped her warm hands around the cold hands of the determined and courageous woman standing in front of her. 'I am glad that you have found the strength to share your agony with me, and, if my words have helped you, then I am truly humbled.' She smiled compassionately. 'Accept all the help that is out there – and there are many organisations that will support you – and draw on the support of any family and close friends you may have. It will be a long and sometimes painful journey, but you are not alone. And you will get there.'

Libby turned to the small pile of books remaining and opened the front page of *The Humble Pawn*. She looked up expectantly, her pen poised.

'I'm giving this copy to one of my dear friends who is suffering. Please could you write a simple message to her.

Something like, *To Rosie, with love.* She will understand…
There is so much power in the words left unsaid, don't
you think?'

As she was leaving the shop Libby called out, 'What is
your name?'

'Emma.'

'Emma, I will hold you in the light.'

She bowed her head in thanks, smiled warmly, and
strode out into the cold.

***

The moment had arrived. The air was heavy, thick with
expectation and intensity. Libby narrowed her eyes to
stare through the sheets of toughened glass that separated
her from the judge and jury. Her hands gripped the edge
of the dock, her fingernails white, her body stiff with
tension. She turned her head to study the coat of arms,
positioned just above the head of the judge. She thought
idly how splendid the ornate wooden-panelled courtroom
was. If only she was here under different circumstances,
she would be able to appreciate the history and the dignity
of the courtroom.

The ruddy face of the judge shone from beneath his
white judicial wig, his eyes twinkling, his demeanour
friendly; for the jury that is, not for the lawyers. He
sympathised with the nervous lead representative of
the jury, a shy Asian man who stuttered over his words.
'Speak slowly, it will help,' he soothed.

'Keep to the point,' he barked at the young but

experienced defence lawyer. 'You are required to inform the jury of the facts. Nothing more.'

She cast her eyes over the jury, a group of people, varying in age from early twenties to late sixties, some Asian, some black and some white Caucasians. It seemed unimaginable that this group of individuals, plucked randomly from the community, would ultimately seal her fate.

The hands of the clock moved unnervingly slowly. She would soon know her destiny. Beads of perspiration formed above her top lip. She stood, her body erect, and she waited. She tried to focus, but the words spoken passed over her head, like driftwood in a raging sea.

After the closing arguments of the lawyers, the jury retired to discuss the case and make their final decision. After an agonising wait, the group slowly filed back to their seats. The judge turned towards them. 'Members of the jury, you have heard all the testimony concerning this case. Have you reached a unanimous decision?'

Silence cut across the courtroom.

The Asian man shuffled uncomfortably. 'We have, Your Honour,' he spluttered.

'And what is that?'

'We found the defendant...'

Her body buckled under her and she fell to the floor.

Epilogue

The tumultuous waves relentlessly batter the jagged coastline, sending powerful jets of spray shooting up towards the sky. The pounding surf cuts through the rocks, like molten lava. I stare into the distance, transfixed by the sheer enormity of the storm.

'*Maman*, isn't it awesome!' the young boy exclaims, pointing to the torrential rain, now lashing against the glass frontage of the apartment. 'It's the Greek god of the sea.' He looks up at me, wide-eyed, his deep-brown eyes boring into mine. 'Poseidon is angry.' He stamps his feet and clenches his fists. 'Did you know that he is called "the deep-sounding earth shaker?"'

I smile at my six-year-old son. 'I didn't know that, Lucus,' I reply, always surprised by the sheer depth of his knowledge of anything to do with the natural world. 'Well, he is certainly shaking the earth tonight!'

Lucus is the spitting image of his father: olive skinned, lean with a strong and muscular physique. His brown hair falls like a thick blanket over his shoulders. He is true to his name: Lucus spelt with a "u" means "forest" or "woodland". He is never happier than when he is skipping in and out of the trees, basket in hand, foraging for wild garlic and myrtle berries. He is drawn to the sea, always combing the beach for natural treasures. Lucus loves books – mostly picture books – about the beauty of the earth. He is a creature of the land, just like his father.

I did return to the vineyard to tell Luca that he had a son, but he had left the region, leaving no forwarding address. Perhaps it is for the best. He is, and always will be, a special part of my life and father to my son.

The storm rages well into the night. I have finally managed to soothe Lucus to sleep, by recounting one of a series of children's stories that I have written: *The Boy, the Forest and the Ocean.*

I return to my rocking chair and contemplate as the eye of the storm rests stubbornly overhead. Having decided to leave England for good five years ago, I bought this coastal apartment just outside Marseille. France is now our home. Here, Lucus can live and breathe the earthiness of the forest and the saltiness of the sea. And it is here that my creative juices flow. I love the freedom to be able to immerse myself fully in the joy of motherhood, and to have the peace and solitude to write. Yes, we are happy here.

Suddenly, the light flashes on and off, finally plunging the apartment into darkness. I fumble for a candle and the matches that I have stored in my desk drawer in case of emergencies. As the flame flickers, orange and yellow, vulnerable in the draught, I reflect on the last few months and years.

My heart aches with sadness as I recall the emotional abuse I suffered at the hands of my husband in Oxford all those years ago; my feelings of confusion, anxiety, shame and guilt. I tried so hard to please Alex, but being constantly undermined with his cruel and callous jibes made me believe it was all my fault. He was right and I was wrong. No one really knows what goes on behind closed doors. Alex had suffered historical abuse – he was damaged – and for that I am sorry, but it didn't give him the right to treat me the way he did. I shudder when I think about the insidious, contradictory and damaging nature of emotional abuse.

After the agonising tragedy in Oxford, my life was never the same again. I was a fugitive: always looking over my shoulder, always on the run. I felt fear, humiliation, anger and grief, but, over time, I discovered the magical and healing qualities of friendship, love and compassion.

I always knew that eventually I would have to return to England and face the music.

I hold images in my head of the courtroom in Oxford; the ruddy face of the judge, the random jury and the terror and humiliation I felt. I smile benignly, knowing that I had got off lightly. In view of my history with no previous convictions, and the circumstances that surrounded my husband's death, judged to be nothing more than a tragic accident, I was given an eighteen-month suspended sentence. The judge issued me with a severe reprimand for concealing the body, and for my subsequent disappearance. I was ordered to complete a gruelling timetable of community service, but I was let off the most strenuous tasks because of my pregnancy.

I stayed in Oxford for a few months, but the city had lost its shine for me; it held too many painful memories.

The house was rapidly sold to the highest bidder, and I whispered my farewells to Oxford, holding sadness, but no regrets.

And so here we are in France. I am the mother of a talented child and a well-respected author and director of my own publishing company, carefully balancing time spent with Lucus and my literary focus. I work tirelessly to provide opportunities for would-be authors, to realise their dreams and to see their stories in print. My creative writing groups give me great pleasure and enable me to give something back to the writing community. I have written several novels, and I like to donate a percentage of my royalties to organisations that provide shelter and refuge for victims of abuse across Britain and France.

I glance over to the coffee table where a chessboard sits: all the pieces standing proud and arranged in their rightful positions. I smile to myself. My life over recent years has been rather like a game of chess. I caress a smooth wooden piece in the palm of my hand. The humble pawn is, in itself, a low-value piece, and yet it holds the hidden strength and power to become a mighty queen. I have been that insignificant pawn: vulnerable, downtrodden and insecure. Over the years, I have developed in confidence, strength and determination. Nothing seems to phase me anymore. I am, at last, capable of being myself and making my own decisions. I am now finally the queen of my empire. But no, it is arrogant of me to suggest that I am a "queen". The title is far too grand. Perhaps instead, I should say that I have become a strong, independent woman, and a dedicated mother to my son, Lucus. Yes,

I make mistakes, I'm certainly not perfect, but together we embrace life and seize all the exciting and creative opportunities that come our way.

The candle diminishes slowly, forming waxen pools at its base. The storm is abating, leaving only the occasional rumble of thunder and flash of lightning, which eerily illuminates the restless sea below.

But everything is not quite right in my world.

The guilt and shame will plague me forever. I relive, yet again, the moments before my husband drew his final breath; the fear in his eyes, the pounding of his chest. Those passing seconds could have been the difference between life and death.

I should have done something. I did nothing.

Acknowledgments

My grateful thanks to:

The amazing team at The Book Guild: Rosie Lowe, Holly Porter and all those who work tirelessly behind the scenes. Thank you for your professionalism, support, guidance and expertise.

Wendy Spray, my life coach, for your invaluable emotional and editorial support, encouragement and precious friendship.

Tanya Street, my motivator, problem solver and friend.

Nathalie, my beautiful French friend, for your advice on language and culture.

My wonderful partner, Dave Glanville, for your endless patience and innovative ideas.

My incredible family for encouraging and supporting my creativity, and for enriching my life in so many ways.

In the end, I take full responsibility for any errors found in this book. The faults are all mine.

Domestic Abuse Contact Information

If you have been affected by issues raised in this book and need support:

Visit the NHS Live Well Domestic Violence and Abuse site.

Women can call the freephone National Domestic Abuse Helpline, run by Refuge on 0808 2000247 for free at any time, day or night. The staff will offer confidential, non-judgemental information and support.

You can also email for support. It is important that you specify when and if it is safe to respond and to which email address:
- women can email helpline@womensaid.org.uk. Staff will respond to your email within five working days
- men can email info@mensadviceline.org.uk
- LGBT+ people can email help@galop.org.uk

The Survivor's Handbook from the charity Women's Aid is free and provides information for women on a wide range of issues, such as housing, money, helping your children, and your legal rights.

If you are worried that you are abusive, you can contact the free Respect helpline on 0808 8024040

For Children and young people affected by mental health issues, visit the Young Minds Mental Health Charity site for support, information and details about local NHS mental health services.

The following twenty-four-hour services are available:
Childline: 0800 1111
The Samaritans: 116123

About the Author

Liz van Santen grew up in Oxford and enjoyed a successful career in education. Passionate about the magical power of creativity, she is also a keen acrobatic dancer and musician. Since retiring, Liz has embraced writing, travelling, sailing, skiing, and spending time with her family. The first book in her duology, *The Humble Pawn*, was published in January 2025, followed by *Queen in the Shadows*, in May 2025. Both books are published by The Book Guild.